THE CROWN OF MISFORTUNE

THE CROWN OF MISFORTUNE

KAITLYN MUELLER

Kaitlyn Mueller

Dedicated to my parents who have always encouraged my creativity. To my Dad, whose creative mind inspired me to want to be like him. And to my Mom, who inspired my love for reading through the bookclubs she started when I was just a child. Incredibly grateful for both of them.

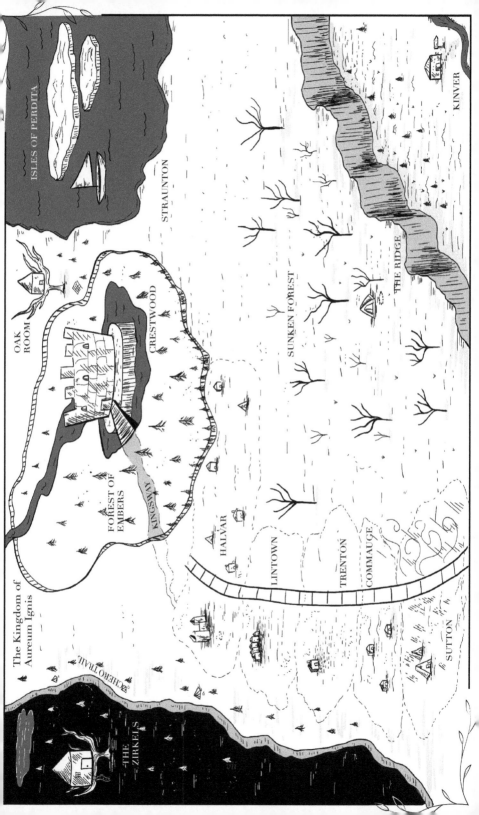

PROLOGUE

The King sat in his chair in the war room. The Kingdom of Aureum Ignis was finally his. He knew this was his destiny, to rule. He looked at the map that stretched out on the table in front of him, showing what was now his.

He knew taking the crown wasn't going to be easy, and he knew it would make him unloved, but he never felt love so he did not care. One month had passed since he took the crown and he already wanted more.

"Frieon," he called out to his top Kingsmen. "Yes, sir, what is it?" Frieon replied, anxiously waiting to hear a response. The King had been on edge lately, everyone could feel it.

"I want to expand our reach. We need to take hold of more land south. Gather an army will you. Find the best Potens that you can and convince them we want them to lead," the King said as he sipped his drink and pushed pieces around on the map.

"Sir, what do you want me to do with the Potens once I've gathered them here?" Frieon said as he stared at the King. They had been friends for years, way before the King had thought to try and take the crown. He patiently waited for further instructions.

"No need to worry about that just yet, I have a plan for them. But really make it seem like you want them in charge, convince them to come to Crestwood, I will take care of the rest."

Frieon nodded and headed out of the war room into the hall. The King stared at the map. He pursed his lips in frustration.

Despite all that he had, he still felt empty.

1

The sun had set just enough below the trees where my surroundings started to glow with the eyes of the creatures of the night. Fireflies sparkled in the distance, small animals started to scurry into their dens and their homes, and I began to make my fire. My campsite wasn't in the most ideal place. Considering I had been traveling for three days' time, I could barely keep my eyes open to put up my tent then try and find the *perfect* spot. I reached down to grab my axe and saw the nearest tree with low hanging dead branches to cut down for wood. I slammed my axe into them one swing at a time for firewood and took the branches over to my campsite. The woods felt quiet, it was nothing I wasn't used to by now. I had lived on my own since I was 15. Being alone wasn't just something I was accustomed to, it was something I craved.

I was never good with fire, it frustrated me and maybe that is why I became a healer rather than anything involved with flame. I put the wood into my fire-ring that I created with small rocks I found nearby. Again, not the most ideal setup, but it would do for now. I grabbed my lighter and started to create a small flame. Come on, this would be much easier if I could just do it without the damn lighter. All the other people at school that were "gifted" could do this with such ease, but not me. Fire was never my forte, and *gifted* doesn't feel like the right word anymore. Cursed does though, or betrayed. I placed old newspapers under the logs and lit them with the lighter. It ignited, but it was damp out so it would need some *help* coaxing it to life. Come on, just light a bit more. I placed my hand near the fire, closed my eyes, and tried to summon a *gift* to help stoke the fire. The flame flickered and went back to its small size. 'COME ON,' I shouted and waved my hands over the fire and it burst into flames throwing me backward and lighting my tent on fire. 'OH HEAVENS, NOT TODAY.' I ran over to the tent and stomped out the flames. It was *singed* but not ruined. A lot of rain might get through the burnt part, but I could patch it later. Thank the heavens. This was no time to lose my tent, not now, not in these circumstances. I couldn't go back if anything went wrong, not now, maybe not ever.

Three days had passed since I had slept well, and if that tent was ruined, I would be pretty angry to have to sleep outside with no protection. Not that the tent was as much physical protection, but the wards I had placed on it kept it hidden. I bought that camping gear last summer from the human wilderness outfitter in town and planned on using it for years to come on many fun adventures. But now I would not go on these adventures, I would use the tent to hide. Everyone thought I was crazy to want to use *human gear,* but they don't understand that I am not the greatest Potens and can't summon all my gifts for every little damn thing. Plus, the brand-new sleeping pad I purchased was state-of-the-art, and who are they to judge comfort?

I sat down on a cut stump next to the fire, placed my hands closer to the flame, not to summon, just for warmth, and looked up at the cracks in the trees where the stars shown through. The Milky Way always looked so beautiful in the middle of nowhere with no light pollution from the surrounding cities. It shown even through the trees. The way it sparkled made me feel at home, even in this wilderness. Home. I had never been anywhere that felt like a real home, I'd been alone for so long, but this momentary feeling must be what it feels like.

I had to be at least 100 miles outside Kinver by now. I had been walking for three days straight, only stopping to eat and quickly rest. I was never the greatest hunter, so I had brought along dried fruit, bison jerky, and protein bars. If I didn't learn to hunt soon, I'd probably starve. But I knew I'd never been able to successfully hunt, so what were the odds that I would be able to do so now. I knew so many Potens who could *will* a squirrel to death with their gifts, but I had never succeeded in that type of gift. Plus, it didn't seem fair to the squirrel, it was not a fair fight.

I grabbed my jerky out of my backpack that my old human neighbor Windy gave to me. She runs a bison farm, and it was the freshest jerky you'll ever find. Windy was human, plain and simple. She was an awesome cook and was always so helpful to me since she knew I was alone. She came by every Saturday to drop off bison jerky to last the full week. I think she must had known that I was never a great cook. I looked down at my tiny fire and my mediocre setup and felt defeated. I noticed a small grouping of mushrooms next to the fire, I picked them up to put them in my bag for later. Mushrooms had great healing properties and could always be useful.

The idea that I still had hundreds of miles to go to reach Havlar was nauseating, but I couldn't go back to Kinver, not after what happened. I looked up at the stars. I wondered if it was getting this bad in Halvar too. Ever since the new King, Jett, was *bestowed on his throne*, it's been a witch-hunt, literally, for the Potens. I was setup. I just know it.

King Jett stole the crown from the old King, killing him while he was sleeping and since that moment, more and more Potens had been accused of killing humans. Potens are never given the time or resources to prove they are innocent, just immediately charged with murder.

My tea could not have harmed or killed someone. But if I stayed, I would have been found guilty. The past three days I had replayed my herbal formula over and over in my head, and there was nothing wrong with it, it had to be a setup. My tea shop was the highest rated in Kinver, my tea was served to royalty, and they think I would poison a commoner? It is not my fault he got sick and died, when he was already really sick. I just don't get it. The tea leaves do nothing without me summoning them to do so. Only a Potens gifted in both herbs and poison could have poisoned my tea. I opened my tea shop four years ago to help the poor of Kinver get better. My tea was always low priced and healed the sick. I could cure anything, even if people were *mostly* dead. That particular human came into my shop every week for three years. He had an illness that caused him great pain. I would make a tea to temporarily ease his pain for the week. His name was Ryon and he showed up every Monday morning waiting for his tea. What happened on that Monday that was different? Why on earth would I kill someone, when the only gift I have was healing and bringing more life into people.

A few hours had passed since I made camp here and it was time to get some sleep. I had another 20 miles to walk tomorrow if I wanted to keep up the pace. I willed the fire to go out, walked over to my tent, unzipped the outside, and crawled in. I took my shoes off, leaving them just outside the tent - close enough to still be under my ward of protection and along with my golden axe. Flipping my human-made headlamp on, I picked up my book on the "Gift of Healing" by my favorite Potens' author, Nora White, and began rereading it for the 50th time.

"You are about to go on a journey through the gift of healing and learn a mountain-full of information on how to heal. *You* are a gift. Your gift is the most powerful thing in the universe, for you can bring full life into things that want to live."

This book was given to me by my mom when she realized I would be a pretty useless Potens without it, considering that my only ability was the gift of healing. Humans in my community appreciated me since I was able to heal their sick loved ones. I brought life to my dying poor community, not death, not ever.

I remember being back in grade school, and Marva laughed at me when I failed every Potens test except the art of healing, "You must be the worst Potens of all time, who only passes *one* exam? Doesn't the average loser at least pass two, you're pathetic." She wasn't wrong though. Those words still ring in my head, but I did end up having the best damn healing tea shop in 800 miles. Probably the best tea shop in all of the Kingdom of Aureum Ignis.

Although Marva works for the rich now, probably creating paintings in seconds with her gifts, it still feels like a success to me that I had my shop, well *had* was the key word there. Nausea took over, who was I now without my shop? That was all I had – all I had ever known. What was I even without that gift, I had nothing else, no family, no hope?

I slammed the book shut, thinking what good would it even do me now when I probably won't ever to be allowed to heal again. I turned off my headlamp, crawled into my 30 + sleeping bag for the chilly night and shut my eyes and instantly drifted off to dream.

2

The sound of rustling leaves woke me. I instantly reached for my pocketknife. I realized it wasn't light out yet, so who the heck was walking through the forest this damn late. I reached over to unzip the tent, and my shoes and my golden axe were missing. Who could see past my wards? The rustling became more distant and I realized they are going to get away. **Not today**. I quickly fabricated some shoes out of extra cloth I brought, willed it together with my gift. These are probably the worst made *magic* shoes anyone has ever seen, but they'll do.

Running through the forest in poorly made shoes with twigs and sticks poking at your feet and being in the dark wasn't the most ideal situation, but I couldn't let this person steal my axe. That golden axe belonged to my grandfather, one of the greatest Potens of all time. He could *will* wood to turn into gold and was the only one known to be able to do it with such precision, that it was unmistakable. In fact, the wood he made into gold was worth more than pure gold itself.

He willed that golden axe for me for my fifth birthday. Grandpa Siron was killed shortly after the new King, Jett came into power.

My grandfather willed wood to gold for the old King and the new one was unfavored by Grandpa so he had him killed so no one could use his gift. But before he did, the King made him will an entire forest to Gold, the Forest of Embers. It still stands, hundreds of miles from here, surrounding the gates of the King's Palace. I hadn't seen too much of my grandfather growing up, since he lived at the castle, but I always knew he loved me.

The new King sent my grandfather's head in a woven box to us after he killed him. That forest he created is said to be cursed in some way though. I had heard so many stories where people who wander into that forest leave confused. They claimed to have lost all of their important, prized possessions that they had with them as they struggled to find their way back home. I always wondered what happened to all of those people, what made them go mad – but it didn't really matter now.

We never did find out why the new King didn't keep Grandpa around. You know, you can't ask a King these questions. Especially a King like this, that threatens death to anyone that does anything slightly different than he wanted. After that moment when we found Grandpa's head in a box, I knew that there was no gift that guaranteed your safety from the King, not even by just being a tea maker.

Sprinting as fast as I could I saw the culprit running in the distance in an old half-ripped sweatshirt with a hood that was visibly frayed. He must be lost to be running in that ripped outfit. I felt sorry for him for a brief moment, the look of his clothes told me he was very poor. But that feeling went right away when I realized I'd have to stop him to get my axe back.

"HEY, THIEF, stop right now or I'll *will* you to death." The hooded person stopped right in their tracks. They put their hands up with one of them holding the axe. "I didn't know you were Potens... sleeping in that, that human made tent." The man slowly turned around. He was tall and he had beautiful blonde hair that was short, but just long enough that you could run your fingers through it. His eyes were as blue as glacier water that I could see shimmering from the distance. "Wait a second, what kind of Potens sleeps in human made tents?" He looked at me with a grin as he put his hands back down as if he was no longer scared. I had to try and make him scared - I needed that axe back.

"Who are you to insult a Potens who just told you she could will you to death?" He looked a little startled and put his arms back up. He spoke with a stutter out of fear that I was actually telling the truth. "LLListen I don't mean no harm, but what the heck are you even doing out here?" he said as he took a step backward.

I took a step closer with my knife in hand. The man slowly lowered his arms so we could talk freely. "I could ask you the same thing, what is a human doing out this far from Kinver? And why are you taking my shoes? There is no way they would even fit you." The man looked at me with disbelief and took a step closer, like he was challenging me saying that I could Will him to death.

"Hold up a second, you just said you are a Potens, you do realize some Potens can will shoes to fit whoever's feet they choose right? My shoes are a bit worn out, and it's not like I had the luxury of buying new ones. I took your axe to trade for the effort to resize these shoes to my feet. By any chance could you do it?" I looked at him with annoyance.

"Let me get this straight, you are trying to trade me *my* axe so I can help you get into *my shoes*? First off, that is the dumbest thing I had ever heard. And second off, I am not that skilled in shoe-making if you couldn't tell..." I looked down to gesture at my feet and looked back up at him to see him smirking. There was no time for this, I needed to use every extra minute to create more space between me and Kinver.

"So please give me back my damn shoes and my axe and leave before I decide to kill you," I said with conviction, being hopeful that I sounded honest. I kept a stern look on my face, trying to be deceiving, trying to convince him that I meant what I was saying. Hopefully he couldn't see through my bluff, I was terrible at willing things to die. I had only willed a beetle to die once, and it didn't even *fully* die, it popped back up to life after a few moments of near-death.

"Listen, I'll make you a deal lady. I keep your axe, I give you back your shoes, and then we go on our way?" Was this guy joking? If I could *will* him to death, I would. "No, that axe is more important to me then the shoes. What do you want? I can create teas that can heal you from sickness, that can make pain go away, that can cure any disease that has come through the doors of my shop. What do you need?" I told him my actual only Potens gift, out of pure desperation, not that he knew it was my only good one. I still had bags of tea leaves in my backpack, and my healing power was admirable to some who had people they loved that were sick.

"Wait, you're Evergreen right? Evergreen from the Tea Shop in Kinver? What was that called, oh Evergreen Rivers Tea? No way?!" He burst into laughter. "You were just accused of killing a man, but there is no way that was you, I mean *look* at you," he said as his head tilted back from laughing so hard. I looked down at myself, I was wearing a zip-up, worn out, grey sweater that I had gotten from an old thrift store, dirty tactical pants that I had sewn patches onto to cover the holes from climbing, and shoes that were made out of pieces of fabric that looked a bit like they were covered in muck.

"I don't have time for this, I have to leave now. Could you just give me my stuff so I can be on my way? Now that you've ruined my sleep, I'll have to start my trek, and I will not leave here without my axe." The man, still laughing, turned around and started walking away. He had no regard to the fact that the axe was all I had left of my family name. My parents left me their small house and the space for my shop, but I could not go back to any of that ever again. "Give me that axe," I said calmly as he continued to walk away from me. "Give me the damn axe," I said a little louder, and he continued to walk away, laughing in the distance. "GIVE ME THE AXE NOW!" I reached out my arms and tried with all my gift and a tree dropped down in his path. Stunned at my own ability, I looked down at my hands. I had never been able to successfully *will* a large object, let alone a tree to fall down. And it was without an axe, and just my gift. I tried not to look stunned, so he might think I can do worse.

The man turned around. "Wow, ok, wasn't expecting that." He started to back away and drop the axe on a pile of leaves on the ground and had his hands up in the air, trying to show me he meant no harm. "Listen I don't want any trouble, just take your stupid axe, but can I ask you one question first?" I walked forward to grab my grandfather's golden axe off the ground. I felt relief once I had it in my hands. "Yes, what do you want?" I looked up at him with disgust, I just wanted to go pack up my tent and supplies and get going. It was later than I thought, or technically earlier considering the sun was about to rise. "Where are you going Evergreen?" he said. I looked at him with disbelief, he was going to try and steal from me and now he wants information? What on earth was that about.

"I'm headed towards Halvar, I am not sure what state Halvar is in, but that is where I am planning on heading." I let out a sigh. I did not want to give away much information, but telling him the direction I was headed did not seem like that bad of an idea, after all, Halvar is the biggest city near here.

"Well, isn't that funny, I'm actually headed that way too. Listen I know I'm human, but I'm the best hunter you'll find for miles. I have my bow and arrow, a machete, and I can kill anything that comes within 300 yards. Why don't we accompany one-another there?" It would be nice to have someone who could get food, considering I don't have much jerky left, and dried fruit isn't going to cut it for the rest of the trip there. But, he did try and steal my things. "You just tried to steal from me, then mocked me for being who I am, and now you want to come with me? You just admitted that you know I am supposed to be arrested for murder. I think going with me would put you in danger, we are better off alone." I looked at him with annoyance. He couldn't be serious.

"Well, yes I did take stuff from you, but let's consider it borrowing since I gave everything back and I can make a deal to make it even. Plus, I'm already in danger, so being with you won't change a thing." I waited to see what he was going to say and gestured for him to keep going. "I'll catch us food now and if I'm not back within the half hour than we go our separate ways. If I am back, we eat and then head out to Halvar together." No one could catch something within a half an hour when we've been making so much noise in the forest, what animal would be that stupid to come out after I made all of that noise by knocking down the tree. I had nothing to lose with this deal. Either he'd come back with fresh food or I got to be alone again, win-win. "Deal," I said with a smirk on my face and I reached out to grab his hand and we shook on it.

I headed back to camp and he headed into the forest. I took off my makeshift muck-covered shoes and put on my hiking shoes that he had stolen. I went into my tent, rolled up my sleeping bag, my sleeping pad, and placed them in my backpack. I grabbed my head-lamp and my book and placed them in my front zipper pocket of my bag. Once I crawled out of my tent, I started to pack up the rain fly, the poles, and the tent itself. I stuffed the tent into its bag and attached it to the bottom of my pack. I heard the sound of an arrow release from its bow in the distance. The human. I rolled my eyes as I continued to put my stuff away. Twenty more minutes went by as I packed fully up, getting ready to win this deal. There would be no way he could get something in this amount of time.

The sun was starting to come up and the sky was a bright pink orange. Leaves rustled in the distance which got louder and louder by the minute. Although I thought it was probably the human, I grabbed my knife and was alert to the noise. I gazed over toward the rustling and saw that thief, carrying a dismembered elk over his shoulder. It was quartered and he was carrying the meat neatly over his shoulder. Disgusting, but I was hungry and incredibly surprised.

"There is no way..." I said under my breath, looking at him with disbelief. He had a full-grown cow-elk. I don't really know how he did it, but my mouth started watering at the sight of it. I was really hungry. "How did you do this so fast?" I wondered as I stared at the sight of the fresh meat. "Practice, lots of practice," he replied.

"Well, let me just clean this, and cook it. We can eat and then we can both be on our way, together. A deal is a deal, right?" he said to me with a grin on his face. He knew he was going to be able to do this before we even made the deal. I had never been more impressed, yet so annoyed in my life. I was grateful though for the food. I rolled my eyes and finished clipping my tent onto the bottom of my pack and take out my lighter to start another fire. "Yes, fine, whatever. A deal is a deal."

3

The sun was rising a bit higher over the tree line and we finished eating the elk. I prayed to the heavens to thank them for the elk, and then we needed to start on our way to Halvar. We had to cook all of it so it wouldn't immediately go bad. I had a few empty bags in my backpack that we could temporarily store the leftover food in, so I quickly put what I could into the bags, the rest would have to be left for the forest. Wasteful, but we did not have the time to worry about that now.

I noticed the human had a small pack with him as well that seemed to be armed with those hunting weapons. This would have been great if we were hunting, but I would have to figure out a way to put some additional wards on my tent so he wouldn't kill me in my sleep.

I was always alone so I had to always be overprepared, constantly running through potential scenarios of bad things that could happen to me. If only I were a better Potens or paid more attention to detail in small enchantments.

I looked over at him with his dirt-covered pants, tan-ripped-sweatshirt and old pack. "What is your name anyways, I'd rather not just address you as 'human." The man laughed, and I rolled my eyes again. I wasn't being funny, I really didn't want to address him as human when I was just accused of killing one. I never viewed humans and Potens to be so different. We're both gifted in different ways. I wanted the human to feel comfortable with me for the long miles ahead of us of our hike. Plus, making him feel like I was letting my guard down might be an advantage to me.

The man said, "I'm Mikka, I'm from Kinver too. I lived down by the Guardian River with my family. I grew up poor as dirt so I hunted and sold anything I could to the Court where the royalty gathers. They never paid much, but it was enough to help support my family." I looked at him as his expression changed, he seemed upset or at least concerned. "Why did you leave Kinver?" I asked inquisitively. He looked down for a moment. "Do you want the truth? If I tell you the truth, our deal still stands," he said.

What on earth was that supposed to mean. "Yes, go on with the truth," I said. Mikka started to speak. "I didn't leave, I was forced to. My sister was accused of stealing from the royals and you know that punishment is death. I offered to serve as a Hunter and live the rest of my life under the Kings' army as long as they wouldn't harm Fern. Fern is my little sister. They agreed, but when they came to get me from my house, they murdered my dad in front of all of us, took the rest of my family, put them in a carriage and handcuffed me. They shoved me in a small trunk in another carriage. When I awoke, I was in the middle of the woods, surrounded by five of the Kings' top hunters, and I saw my pack with my weapons in it and they were playing target practice with my bow against a tree.

"They had told me they were going to kill the rest of my family. They said I would serve as a Hunter for the King, but I would be *willed* to do so by his most powerful Potens, Sir Frieon. I had to do something, I needed to get back to my family.

"They didn't know I always keep a knife hidden in the side of my shoe. They hadn't checked, so I slashed the hunter's throats when they slept that night and took my pack and ran. I've been running through the woods for three weeks now, trying to come up with a plan of where to find Fern and my mother. I had headed back to Kinver, but they weren't there, so I was retracing my steps to Halvar. I just pray to the Heavens that they are still alive," he said.

I used to feel something when people shared stories like this, but it happened so frequently now I felt quite numb to it all. I was not surprised at this point, our society was crumbling. The new King had these crazy ulterior motives and was using everyone he could to increase his power. The new King seemed like he was afraid of Potens and created new specific boundaries that the Potens had to abide by.

The three rules were: No killing whatsoever under penalty of death (unless by the King's orders), no using gifts for an advantage against others under penalty of death, and no unregistered Potens under penalty of death. We had to sign our names on a sheet and got a specific registry number that was added to our informational identification cards. Death seemed to always be the punishment for breaking any of those rules. No trial, no witnesses, just death. They never even gave people time to explain what had happened.

I wasn't really sure what to say to Mikka. I was certain he wanted some sort of comfort, but I was not going to be that person for him. "I'm so sorry to hear about your dad Mikka, and the rest of your family. I know there has been so much death recently, but I don't know how you'd get them back from the King. The Castle was guarded by the best Potens out there and was surrounded by the Forest of Embers which at this point is impossible. Not to mention what you would do after you got to them. How would you even get out? What do you think you are going to do?"

I felt angry at the state of our Kingdom. I used to have such pride for what we stood for - the peaceful living and collaboration between human and Potens alike. Now, it was all crumbling. I couldn't believe this was the way our society was headed. I looked down at my shoes instead of at Mikka as we both continued to walk onward. I did not have much more to say. I had been alone for so long and had lost everyone I loved to this King. There was no faith left for me. He couldn't answer my question and he just looked up at the sky.

After a while of walking, I stepped a little closer to him and said "My parents were also killed by the King a while ago. I was 15 when I became an orphan. My dad was human too and My mom was a Potens, gifted in willing water. She could will water to make shapes and she could make the water dance beautifully. It was such a beautiful gift. She had performed several shows for the King. She too was beautiful, just like her gift. She had long beautiful black hair and the most emerald green eyes I've ever seen.

"My dad was a wood worker, he worked as an apprentice in a Potens shop helping however he could, he was talented and able to keep up with even the finest Potens. He thought my mom was beautiful. The problem was the King also thought my mom was beautiful." I paused for a moment. It was after all her beauty that got them both killed.

"My parents were both sentenced to death when my mom wouldn't accept the King's advances. She loved my father with her whole heart. I was 15 when they both were killed. The King's Guard came by and killed my father first to punish her and then her for not giving into his desires. I had been living on my own since." I hadn't said that out loud in so long, I always just told people I was alone rather than explain the why behind it all.

I felt really awkward telling people my story, it just seemed stupid. It was all done now, and I had to deal with the consequences for a long time. I did not expect anyone to ever feel bad for me. When you tell people your secrets, it made you vulnerable, and I didn't like being vulnerable. I, of course, never share the part of the story where

I was there when it all happened, hiding behind a chair in the living room. I held my mom as she took her last breath. Mikka looked at me with a blank stare, I think he was also very unsure of what to say.

"Evergreen, I am sorry that your parents were killed – I can't imagine what that must have been like for you, and then to be completely alone must have been really hard. This is going to keep happening to more people if we just accept it rather than do something about it. I know deep down my family is still alive, and I might just be human, but I can *kill*, and I *will kill* anyone who stands between me and getting my family back." Mikka looked down at the dirt as we kept walking. I did not think he was right. We were safer just avoiding the law rather than trying to challenge it. I did not want to get in more trouble that I already was.

We walked in silence for the next few hours. I did feel guilty about feeling hopeless since my whole life has been about survival on my own. The reality of this world was harsh. No one was stronger than the Potens at the palace and any highly battle-skilled Potens had been recruited by the royal army. You'd need a miracle to get past them to even see the King, let alone have the opportunity to kill him.

The Kings Guard was powerful as well. It made it difficult to even get in front of the King unless you were being sentenced to death. The new King was human and would always claim he was doing what was right to keep peace and order in the country. At least that is what he told everyone in the beginning. The problem was he used his privilege to break rules and killed many without real cause. After he had "claimed" the throne, he had made Potens everywhere scared of stepping, even a toe out-of-line. We were all frightened of what could happen, I mean, look what had happened to me. Even Mikka, a human, was afraid of what the King was capable of. Choosing to rule by fear has been effective for him so far.

After what felt like ten long very quiet hours of hiking through the forest, we came upon a small stream that wrapped around this beautiful oak tree. The noise of the stream was loud enough to break the silent tension between us.

There was a patch of flat land next to it with mossy ground which looked like it would be comfortable to sleep on. Around the area were a bunch of good-sized rocks to make a fire ring. The area would be a great campsite for now and we needed to rest up after such a long day hiking.

The sun had just set, leaving a light glow on the forest that was just enough light to set up our camp without needing the headlamp just yet.

"Mikka, I'll start to put the fire together, if you want to go pre-pare dinner." Mikka nodded back at me and grabbed the food we had from the bags and started putting everything out on a rock to get ready to cook once the fire was on.

The quieter it had been between us, the guiltier I felt for not hav-ing been as sensitive to what he had gone through. I had felt so de-feated for so long by King Jett. I had lost everything, my family, my tea shop, my reputation. It didn't feel like anything would ever im-prove. It had been this way almost my whole life and I was feeling utterly and completely hopeless. I wanted to tell him I was sorry and that I was sure it would get better, but the truth was I was not sure it would ever get better. At least it wasn't like there was anything we could do about it.

I started to put together a small fire ring with rocks from the stream. I pulled rock by rock from the stream to stack them one by one in a circle. I didn't really care if it looked nice, just that we wouldn't burn the whole forest down. I chopped down dead wood off nearby trees with my golden axe and brought that wood over to the fire. I stacked the logs on top of one another in a square pat-tern. Thankfully, the logs were dry this time. I looked around the campsite and grabbed some dead grass and small twigs to get the fire started. I didn't use my gift this time, I felt too defeated and exhausted to even try, so I rubbed two sticks together to get the fire going. It surprisingly did not take long. I think I was really motivated to get warm. Once the fire was going, I sat down for a moment to relax.

Mikka came back over to the fire with the food he was prepping. We heated up some of the leftover meat that we had yesterday – we couldn't keep it for long without it going bad so we might as well enjoy a feast. Mikka placed the thin rock slab over the fire like a make-shift grill and started to heat up the meat. I was really thankful for meat after having gone a few days without any. Not being able to hunt really put me at a disadvantage.

You could hear the birds chirping and starting to settle into their nests as the night fell around us. The sound of the leaves moving from the wind was loud enough to continue the white noise as were the small animal noises from far away. We could hear the howls of wolves getting ready for the night, but not one word from Mikka or myself. The silence between us was deafening, but I always felt like I wasn't alone with the sounds of the forest. Since I spent most of my life outside of the tea shop alone, the silence did not usually bother me. This time though, I didn't know what to say and I felt uncomfortable.

Over the crackling of the fire, I decided to end the silence, "Mikka listen, I didn't mean what I said earlier, you could probably find a way to get your family back, I have just been so down on myself from everything that has happened to me and my family from King Jett, it hasn't been easy. I think you should try to get them back, but I think it is a death sentence trying to break into the castle. I am just saying you should be careful, come up with a plan and don't do anything irrational." Mikka looked at me with surprise. He sat back trying to get comfortable as he spoke. "I know you were probably right earlier, but I appreciate you saying that. I probably won't be able to get them back, but I am going to try even if it means my death. I am nothing without my family and I will go until I cannot go anymore to try and bring them to safety. The corrupted King has got to be stopped and the way this is going, Potens are going to end up back in chains like they were long ago if he remains our King."

The word *chains* sent a chill down my spine. When I was little, my parents used to tell me stories like that. They would tell me how years ago, the King would enslave all the Potens and put them under Night-chains which allowed their gifts to be drained and used by powerful humans. We had come a long way from that since then, but the corruption still exists in our Royals, now more than ever.

"Yes, it is bad, but there are so many people on the King's side at this point, I'm not sure how it will ever change. I didn't even get a fair trial when I was accused of killing that man. I was simply accused, and they burned down my shop, and I grabbed what I could and left before they killed me too. Mikka, this King needs to be stopped, you are definitely right, but I am not nearly powerful enough to help you. My gift is in healing, not battle of any sort. I'll take you to Halvar, but I am not looking for a fight, I am simply looking to prove that I am innocent and start over." I did not want to get in any more trouble. I could simply help him on his way and then we could part ways from there.

I did not have a death wish, I wanted to prove my innocence. I wanted to buy a new shop and get set up in a new town. After I had proved my innocence, only then could I find out how I was framed. I did not want to involve myself further in the King's corrupted actions now – I had been through enough and I wanted to live a quiet, unbothered life.

The truth was, I was on my way to a new town because I had friends in Halvar, Potens with powerful gifts. I could change my name there and apprentice at their shops for now, posed as a human until I was able to find out who set me up. I did indeed want revenge, but I had given up on that thought. I needed to start over, gather resources and true friends that would help me prove my innocence.

But who set me up? I had that tea shop for four years now, healing anyone that walked through my door, I had done nothing but help Kinver thrive by healing the sick, healing the Potens that were ungifted in healing. I healed humans and healed people's sick animals. I hadn't done anything that warranted questioning.

My life had changed yet again when that man stepped into my shop one week ago. I drafted him a simple Nash-tea that could help his long-term illness and willed the tea leaves to heal him. I did what I always did, boiled the water, willed the tea with the proper leaves and herbs and stirred it three times. I handed the tea to the man so he could heal, and he walked out the door. I heard a thud and walked out to see what happened and the man had dropped dead the second he walked out of my shop after a sip of the tea. I was sick to my stomach after seeing him. I ran to the nearest Guard and told him that the man died and immediately was accused of killing him. If I'd had known they were going to accuse me, I would have moved his body somewhere else first before reporting him dead – but I can't really worry about should-haves now. There isn't any point. What's done is done.

I interrupted the crackling of the fire and the slight popping of the meat on the rock. "Mikka I do have some friends in Halvar, maybe they can help you with where to go next, or at least give you some more supplies for your journey. I know they have a lot of connections and friends all over so they might be able to point you in the right direction at least." I looked down at the cooked meat. I felt grateful for Mikka otherwise I would be eating some dried fruit, again.

Mikka looked up at me after taking a bite of his food. "I would be grateful if you could bring me to someone who can help. I am not asking for you to come with me, but if you have resources I could use to get there, I would be in debt to you. Anything would help so I can try and save my family."

I smiled at him and nodded, and we sat in silence for the rest of the night. Mikka took the food off of the fire and rested it on another large rock next to us. We waited for it to cool down a bit before cutting the meat apart with my knife in order to share it. I didn't bring proper utensils so this would have to do. The fire crackled and the stars shone through the forest canopy above. If we hadn't been running from death, I'd say it was pretty beautiful here. We both sat and looked at the stars for a bit before getting ready to sleep. We'd have a long journey ahead of us tomorrow, and we would need to get a good night's rest.

I still didn't trust him though, so I had my knife close to me on my belt. I felt sorry for him, but he was after all a thief, who is to say he was not also a liar? I wasn't one to just trust people, they had to earn it, and Mikka started our encounter off in a way that I wouldn't be able to trust him just yet.

He had a small blanket in his pack that he laid down on the mossy grass so he could fall asleep next to the fire. Without any element protection, it made sense that he wanted to sleep next to the warmth of the flames. I however, set up my tent farther away and I willed my tent to protect me, from anything, even Mikka. Not that the wards helped me last time. I must not have done them right.

I crawled into my tent and I zipped up my tent from the inside. This time I would not make the same mistake and brought my axe inside with me. No more risks, no more stupid mistakes. I laid down in my sleeping bag, turned my headlamp on and continued reading 'The gift of healing'.

Page 58: 'Tea is a great way to cure human-born illnesses. The most common cure is the Nash-Tea, which is the best option for curing the flu and relieving pain for long-term illnesses. After the patient drinks it, they will be cured of the flu within 60 seconds of their first sip.

1. Take dried leaves of basil, and leaves of a fall maple, and crush them into pieces

2. Place the leaves in a pot filled with simmering water

3. Add three full cinnamon sticks to the water

4. Add four drops of organic honey

5. Boil this mixture for 45 minutes, add a spoonful of cardamom, (made with the gift of healing)

6. Will the mixture to heal, bring out the life force in these ingredients

7. Serve warm, (best served with a home-made ginger snap for flavor)

I had read this mixture at least 100 times and I could make this tea with my eyes closed. I did not poison that man. I had to prove my innocence somehow. I had to get my tea shop back. I just wanted my life back. It wasn't special, but it was quiet, and it was the way I've been living for the last few years.

I closed the book shut and turned my headlamp off. I tried to get comfortable, but the events of the day prevented me from finding a way to do so. There was so much to think about, but eventually I drifted off to sleep.

The sun's warmth woke me in my tent. I felt the rays shining through and that meant it was later than I wanted it to be. We needed to get started on our day. We should have headed out much earlier. I had slept with my axe in my tent, fearful that Mikka *the thief* would try and take it while I slept. I reached for it under my pillow and held it in my hand as I unzipped my tent and walked over to the fire-ring and noticed Mikka's pack wasn't there. Mikka was actually nowhere to be found. The panic set in, I was fearful that he had left with my stuff. I quickly ran over to my pack and started rummaging through it to see if he had taken anything when his voice came from behind me.

"Think I would have tried to steal from you again Potens?" Mikka laughed and was right behind me with breakfast over his shoulder. He was smiling because it was very clear that I did not trust him. "I didn't even hear you sneak up on me, I always hear everything." I was worried, no one had ever just snuck up on me like that.

He was right though, I did not trust him, not for one second. I wasn't about to just let my guard down now. Mikka put breakfast down and started to work on getting it prepared. He didn't look up. "I hunt Evergreen, sneaking up on things is what I do best. It is how my family was able to survive," he said. He had a point. I just didn't want to come off as vulnerable.

He continued working to get breakfast ready for us to eat before we headed out for another long trek. "I'm trying to keep up with my end of the deal, but you have to trust me a little bit here – I don't think you would have been able to make it on your own without being able to hunt, you look so thin from not eating enough." He was right *again*, in the last few days that I had been in hiding and then camping in the woods I hadn't had any real meals until he came along. He continued to prepare breakfast as I packed up my tent.

We needed to make it to Halvar in one week to meet my friends that were waiting for me. I was able to get word to them that I would be headed there then. Tomorrow we would have to make the ascent up Mount Ridge and climbing a mountain face of 200+ feet with someone I barely know let alone trust at all, did not seem like an ideal situation. I felt safer alone. Climbing with him was a risk, but one I would have no choice but to take. The idea of having to put a little trust in him made me nervous but realistically it was probably safer to make the trek with someone than to go it alone.

Mikka and I had breakfast. I pulled out the map I had brought of the Sunken Forest Trails and we plotted out our route towards Halvar. "So, if we go up the Ridge, we can shorten our trip by four days, but you don't have climbing gear I'm assuming? Right?"

Mikka looked at me with a grin and reached into his pack and pulled out a really worn-out harness and some very old climbing gear. "I sometimes climb to get above the animals when I hunt, I found this harness in back in Kinver years ago. I don't have money to buy one myself, so it works for the time being. It hasn't broken on me yet." I looked at his harness with shock. Who the heck climbs with a worn out, *torn* old harness? I would rather try and free climb than try and use that old thing. There was no way anyone could trust that to actually support their weight if they fell.

I grabbed ahold of his harness and his rusty old gear and looked it over. I handed it back to him with disgust written on my face. This will have to do. We didn't have the four extra days to waste by going around the ridge. Plus, my friends would only be in Halvar for a little while - I didn't want to take the chance in missing them. I was just glad I wasn't going to be the one wearing that harness. This human is either really brave, or really stupid to be using this climbing gear but either way, we needed to make that climb.

I looked at the map and then back up at Mikka. "I will be the one to lead the climb, once I get to the top, I'll secure the rope and you can climb up. After we've ascended the Ridge, we'd have about a three-day trek to the edge of Halvar, unless we stop in Sutton at the edge of the Sunken Forest and take the train to Halvar, which would shorten our trip by two days. I just don't know if anyone in Sutton has been alerted that I ran out of Kinver, or you having escaped so it could be quite risky," I said.

I wondered which option would be best with all things considered. It was hard enough when it was just me to worry about, but Mikka must be currently hunted down by the Kings Guard since he killed some of them. I looked down at the map trying to find another way, but if we didn't go into Sutton, our trip would be longer. The edge of the Sunken Forest was known for its crazy monsoons which we really did not have the equipment to deal with. The wind started to pick up and as I was holding my map the wind tore the edge a bit. I looked up and the sky was changing fast from sunny skies to darker clouds.

"Ok I think that signals it is time to go. Now that it's going to rain, I'll pack up the rest of the gear, and you put away any extra food we have since I doubt we can hunt something later today. We will have to take the ascent up the Ridge, the rain is already going to push us back as it will take some time to climb," I said. Mikka looked over at me and nodded quickly in acknowledgement. "Well, I guess that's the plan then. Let's hurry up so we can avoid getting most of our stuff soaked," he said.

He started to put the food into the only storage container we had which was small but having some food stored for later rather than none was better. I started to put our things into the respective bags and clipped the tent to the bottom of my pack. It started to drizzle around us.

The rain hitting the crackly leaves on the ground sounded magical and I felt like it transported me back in time for a moment to better days. I had always loved the rain and by being out in nature, just for a moment, I felt a small glimmer of what used to be. We used to have a summer cabin that we went to for family trips when I was really little, and I always loved to sit on the covered porch and listen to the rainfall with my mom and dad. My dad would watch as my mom shifted the raindrops into beautiful patterns with her gift and I would try my hardest to do what she did, but I was only successful in changing the direction of the rain. You could only see the change I made if you tilted your head to the side and looked really hard.

I snapped out of it. I couldn't be thinking about the past like that, not anymore. I looked up and the clouds were moving in fast, darkening the sky. I grabbed an old rain coat out of my bag – it had burn marks on it from when I almost set myself on fire trying to use my gift. I put it on and placed my axe in the side pocket of my backpack for safekeeping and zipped up my pack.

"We need to hurry, we have at least 15 miles to hike before sundown," I shouted towards Mikka. He was putting his pack together with the extra food and grabbed a small sweater out of his pack. "You don't have any rain gear?" He looked at me with annoyance. "I told you I was poor right? I didn't have money for a nice coat, everything I have is either stolen or given to me. I've always just made do with whatever we had. I'll be fine. Running from the Kings Guard hasn't granted me a bunch of time to go shopping either. It's not like there is a store in the middle of the woods." He smirked at me. "C'mon we have to hurry," I shouted as I realized how silly that question actually was.

The rain continued to pour harder and harder around us, but we still hiked through. We had no choice. We would run out of time if we stopped now. My boots were water resistant and not waterproof, so my socks were starting to feel soaked on the inside of my boots – it felt squishy with each step forward. I started to have chills from the wind picking up. We had to get to the Ridge by sundown if we wanted to scope out the ascent tonight to make it easier for us to-morrow. I wanted to plan out the route we could try and take, and I was hopeful that we could do that tonight.

The King

B ack at the castle the King sat at his desk rummaging through books and books trying to find the answer. "I just don't understand. I have the power, why are the things I am trying to accomplish not working?" the King said in frustration to the hooded man in the room. "Find me answers. *She* knows the answers. You can find out. You must find out or the deal is off." The hooded figure stood up and walked toward the desk.

"My King, there must be another way. We can try and get to the Isles of Perdita. The answers to our problems lie there." The King put the books down for a moment to look up at the hooded figure. "Find the answers from her first. Then we can go to the Isle." The hooded figure nodded and started to walk away. "Oh, and make sure there are two guards on Fern's door day and night, we can't risk losing her too," the King said to the hooded figure as he disappeared through the shadows of the castle hall.

The King picked up the books once again and continued to read through them, desperate to find the answers he was searching for.

6

The rain had stopped halfway through the day, leaving both of us drenched as we trekked through the rest of the forest. Although the sun had slightly dried some of our clothes, our feet were still soaked. The sun was starting to fully set, and we had about a little over a mile to go and could finally see the ridge from here. We were both still sopping wet from the rain all morning through the afternoon, and the sun going down was making the wind a bit unbearable. Once we got about 50 feet out from the Ridge, we stopped to take a look at the wall and plan our route. I pointed up to one section of the rock. "See that mossy section about halfway up the face of the ridge? Well, right next to that looks like a good place to break since it looks like a small cave or something. If we make it to there, we're good to go the rest of the way up. It looks a bit easier after that part. I think if we take it slow, we should be ok."

Mikka nodded but interrupted anyways. "Can't you just *will* your way to the top." I rolled my eyes. Why would he think I wouldn't announce that as an option if it were possible? If I could just will my way to the top, I would have willed him to shut up with all the damn Potens questions. It was getting old. "No, I don't have that kind of gift, although that would be great right now." Mikka seemed to have understood that I was annoyed.

I was eager to change the subject when Mikka interrupted my thought. "Do you climb often?" he said. We both tried to dry ourselves off a bit. "I've always really loved climbing, and admired humans that do it. It takes some courage to just climb up something with the risk they take of falling, but they do it anyways with no gifts, no healers, just themselves. I actually learned to climb from someone who walked into my shop with no way to pay for the healing draught they needed. Someone had poisoned them after they had stolen from them in poker, so they had nothing left, and he had only a few hours to live.

"I gave him the tea but this time for a trade. I wanted to learn something new, so he taught me to climb." I was always so thankful that I met that human because after that moment, climbing became something I loved – although I think this experience would be entirely different now that my life truly does depend on it. Climbing was a way for me to forget about the troubles I had been through and work on solving a problem as I found my route up the wall. It was a great stress reliever and helped me find focus in my life.

We looked at the wall for a few more moments as we picked our route. Then we headed onward. We walked a little faster and headed for the very bottom of the ridge. The sun was setting just below the tree line, so it was getting darker faster, leaving an orange-pink glow about the forest just before it set into black. The darkness began to quickly surround us.

I threw down my pack. "Let's set up camp here, tomorrow at sunrise I'll start my climb. Don't worry about hunting tonight, we can eat this morning's leftovers, and I have dried apricots we can share." I started to unzip my pack and grabbed out the apricots and threw them over to where we would set up our fire. Mikka started to put together a fire ring, and I grabbed my bags of tea leaves. I had a small pot in my pack, so I took that out, poured some water in it from my bottle, and started to put the tea leaves in. "What are you making?" Mikka looked over at me as I was willing the leaves to work. He was shivering from being wet and the wind blowing. "We've been in the cold all day, we could get sick, and if I get sick, I have no way of healing you. I'm making a Cooling-Tea, it's preventative for cold like symptoms. I was going to offer you some but knowing my *reputation* I doubt you'd even want it anyway." I was sort of joking, but at the same time, who is going to want to drink my teas if they thought I had killed someone with them? Mikka looked over with a smile and said, "I doubt you could even hurt a fly, I'm sure the tea is fine, and I'll have some because it's cold anyways. It would be nice to have warm tea right now." Mikka looked back down toward the fire ring and walked away to gather some wood.

I spent most of my time alone, so this was the most time I had spent with another person in years. I never relied on anyone and this was really testing my patience and my willingness to share, I felt vulnerable like this. I hated feeling vulnerable. I always buried my feelings to prevent having uncomfortable conversations and this, this felt very exposed.

Even my friends I had become fairly distant with, except of course Tresa and Barth. Thinking about them made me so happy that in a few days' time I would get to see them again. It had been so long since they left on their full-time trip. They were both Potens, with such incredible gifts.

Tresa could manipulate objects of any sort. She could snap her fingers and an entire forest would fall. But Tresa was gentle and her gift was destructive. She preferred to use her gift to will things together instead of apart, so she made the most beautiful furniture. Barth was gifted in transformations. He could transform a bug into a lion, a cat into a tiger, even himself into whatever he pleased. Both he and Tresa gave up working in a Potens job for the people and they pretended to be human instead. A few of their friends and family were accused of killing humans, so out of fear they moved to hide among them – pretending to be human. They bought a carriage about a year ago so they could head off on the road. They even asked me to join but I couldn't leave my shop, it was the only thing I had left in my life that felt solid, so they left, and I stayed in Kinver. Halvar was the biggest city in our area. It was a good place to go if you wanted to pretend to be someone new which was why it would be the perfect place for me right now.

I grabbed the lighter and headed over toward the wood piles Mikka had created, placed them in the fire-ring, and willed the spark to catch bigger flames. With the wood being damp, I had to try and use my gift to make the spark. I never was the greatest with fires, so it took longer than I wanted it to. Once the fire was roaring, I grabbed my tea pot, and boiled the tea water. Once the water was bubbling, I grabbed a small mug out of my pack and poured the tea into the mug. I took two sips. It smelled like burning wood, and dark cherry chocolate. I looked up at Mikka who had sat down on the other side of the fire. "Here, have a sip, it only takes one sip for it to work." I only had the one mug, so I handed the mug over to Mikka, and he looked up and me, then down at the mug, then back up at me. "I've never had any healing tea before." Mikka took a sip and I could see his expression change. "This is way better then I imagined it to be, it takes like cherry hot cocoa." Mikka smiled and had another sip as he tried to get warm from the cold rainy journey from today.

We sat around the fire for another hour and laid our top layers and sweatshirts on a tree branch close enough to the fire to dry overnight. The moon was full tonight which lit up our surroundings, making the night easy to see in and maneuver around. I always loved the full moon as it shone brightly in the sky.

"Mikka, I don't mean to keep bringing this up, but how did you plan on getting your mom and sister back?" I looked down at the fire so it would avoid the awkward stare. "I haven't quite figured that out yet. I don't have that many contacts, but I do know I'm a pretty good hunter, and resourceful. When I get to the gate I'll figure out a plan, until then I'm taking it day by day until I'm closer to them or until I have a plan figured out," he said. Mikka looked down at the bag of dried apricots, opened it and had a few as he sat there thinking. I wasn't really sure what to say, the Forest of Embers that blocks the Palace is difficult enough to navigate, let alone if you get past it, I've heard it is pretty much a death sentence for trespassing. I had never been past the edge of the Forest of Embers, so past it was all unknown territory for me.

"Well like I said, if we make it to Halvar, my friends might have somewhere you can go or maybe some advice to help you on your way," I said. Mikka gave me a small grin and nodded his head as if to say thanks but he seemed too deep in thought. We both were exhausted from the long journey today and had another really long day ahead of us tomorrow.

After we ate, we both started to get ready for bed. I quickly put up my tent and got my sleeping bag out. I looked at Mikka and nodded as if to say goodnight before I started to head into my tent. Mikka laid out a blanket on the forest floor, although it was cold, he wouldn't get sick because we drank the healing teas. The warmth of the fire and the tea helped me feel a little better from the cold, windy day.

The forest felt silent other than the small drops of rain that were still falling off the leaves of the trees above as well as the crackle of the fire outside the tent. As I laid down in my tent, I thought about all of the possible terrible outcomes of the climb tomorrow, and the fact that I would have to fully trust Mikka with my life and I had only known him for a few days. I placed the axe underneath my pillow, made sure my wards were still in place. My mind raced until I finally fell asleep.

7

Birds started to chirp as the sun started to peak up over the horizon. I heard a noise outside of my tent. I rushed to get out of my sleeping bag and grabbed my axe and quickly unzipped my tent and popped my head out to see what it was. It was just Mikka yet again, who was putting his things together and back in his pack. "Oh, hello there sleepy. I was going to wake you up if you didn't get up by the time I was done," Mikka said to me. I must have looked half asleep. I slowly stepped out of my tent with my axe and started to pack up my things. Mikka was eating some of the dried apricots and sitting on a dead tree stump as I finished to put the last few things in my pack. I grabbed a handful of the dried apricots, had a drink of water, and looked up the Ridge.

We spent the next few moments packing up the tent, the food, and all of our stuff to be hooked onto our packs securely. I strapped the tent onto the bottom of the pack again and braced myself for what was to come. We'd have to climb with our gear on. I made sure that everything was tight and wouldn't fall off as I moved around.

We silently walked over to the wall and put our stuff down to get the harnesses on. "Ok Mikka, are you ready?" I looked over at him and he looked so tired. "As ready as I'll ever be," Mikka said back as he started to slowly put on his climbing harness.

I grabbed my harness, slid one leg into each hole, and secured the harness tight around my waist. I pulled on it twice to make sure it was snug and that it wouldn't move too much if I fell. We both walked over to the very bottom of the ridge and I started to unravel the rope. Attaching the rope to my belt, I secured the knot and then paused for a moment. We were dead if we didn't do this right. I did not have the 'right' gifts to help us here.

"Here." I tossed the other end of the rope to Mikka. "I'll start the ascent, once I'm at that hold near the moss, I'll yell down, and you can start to climb up. If anything goes wrong...." My voice trailed off. There could not be any mistakes here, we were running out of time and could not afford to be pushed back farther.

I was nervous as heck to climb this Ridge. The realization that if we did not do this right and something happened to one of us would mean that we were both dead because we couldn't go to a hospital without being caught. I looked up the face of the Ridge and immediately felt nauseated. Climbing usually made me feel less stressed, but today with everything that was at stake, it was the last thing I wanted to do. I tried to put all the negative thoughts out of my mind, but it was always something I had to deal with – anxiety. I had no choice but to force the adrenaline to kick in, forcing the anxiety to the side for a little while.

Mikka must have picked up on my energy shift. "Evergreen, I could climb it first if you wanted," he said. That would make things easier on me, but I don't know if I can trust him. Having to trust him being the one to pull me up, I just couldn't take that risk. I could not let my anxiety get in the way of me getting safely to the top. "No, I'll go." I was sure this was the right decision.

I placed my hands against the rock, feeling the surface. Thankfully it mostly dried overnight. I grabbed onto the side of the rock with my fingertips, found a small step to place my foot, and lifted myself off the ground. I was going to take this slowly and just work on one tiny step at a time. I started to climb, hand, foot, foot, hand, press up, hand, foot, hand, press up. I thought about nothing except where the next handhold would be. Usually, I was climbing for sport, where if I fell I would be connected to the wall. But this, this was way different. I wasn't connected to the wall, the only reason I was even wearing the harness was so that I could pull Mikka up with the rope or at least be able to make his fall less lethal. The rope and harness did nothing for me right now.

I tried not to think about the reality of free climbing this ridiculous wall and continued to climb. I had to also trust that he wasn't going to try and pull me down. I pushed that thought out of my head and continued. Hand, foot, foot, hand, press up. I only looked up at the rocks above, thankfully this part of the wall was pretty rigid, making it easier to grab onto.

I put my hand in my old chalk bag that was attached to my belt so it would be easier to grip the wall. Hand, foot, foot, hand, press up. This would be much easier if I didn't have this heavy backpack on. The next 20 minutes went by so slowly as I was pulling myself up this wall. I kept thinking that death awaited me if I made one mistake.

Hand, foot, foot, hand, press up. About three feet from the small hole in the wall next to the moss, I grabbed onto a small hand hold in the rock. The rock suddenly broke loose from the wall and I started to fall. My left hand grabbed on as tight as I could to the wall, gripping with all of my fingertips as I tried to swing myself close enough to the wall to keep hanging on. A few rocks tumbled down the wall, and then all was still.

Mikka yelled up at me. "Ever are you alright?" I didn't answer immediately. My life had just flashed before my eyes, am I alright, *heck no*. I gripped the wall with my left fingertips and re-gripped the wall in a new ridge in the rock with my right hand. Once I had my balance, I yelled back down to Mikka. "Yea, I'll be fine, just a few more steps up." I glared above at the hole in the wall. 'Ok Ever you can do this, just a few more steps, and you're safe. C'mon.' I whispered to myself for encouragement, I did that a lot.

I grabbed more chalk out of my bag and started to climb. Hand, foot, foot, hand, press up. After what felt like another thirty minutes that was probably only ten minutes, I grabbed onto the shelf in the wall that was a small cave and pulled myself up.

I untied the rope from my harness and tied it onto a rock nearby so Mikka would be safe if he needed the rope. As he climbed, I could wrap more of the rope around the rock, so he would be able to pull himself up or soften his fall from falling all the way back down to the bottom. I looked down at the face of the rock wall and felt really accomplished. It was like a wave of anxiety was lifted off of my shoulders. I had always been a good climber, but never thought I would have to free climb a wall with no backup plan and a backpack weighing me down.

Once I was able to catch my breath, I signaled for Mikka. "Ok Mikka, you can start climbing!" I shouted down towards him and he nodded back. Mikka started his ascent. Mikka got to the hole in the wall with no problems and faster than I got there. 'Show-off.' I helped pull Mikka up into the small cave, and we sat for a little while to rest.

Mikka started detaching the rope from his harness. He rewrapped the rope around a rock, and he helped me attach the rope to my harness. This way, if I fell, it wouldn't be all the way to the ground, this was my safety net this time. "Ok, this actually looks much steeper than I thought, but at least this time we have some sort of break to catch our breath and rest our bodies. I'll go to the top, just like last time, but once I get to the top, unwrap the rope and attach it to your harness and I'll tie it off to a tree at the top."

Mikka gave me a smirk, which I was unsure of why. "Ok Ever, whatever you say. So *bossy*." He turned around and grabbed my pack and handed it to me. Maybe I was still being a bit bossy. Oh well, he'll get over it. As I told him, I wasn't used to having company for this long. I did things the way that I wanted to, when I wanted to.

I prepped for the next part and put my pack on my back. Climbing with a backpack felt nerve racking as ever, it added so much extra weight and made me feel so off balance. I had to push that intrusive thought of falling out of my head, now was not the time to worry.

"Ok Ever, you can do this," I said to myself quietly before I started to climb. I put my hand in the chalk bag and started my ascent as I slipped out of the cave and onto the cold rock wall once more.

Hand, foot, foot, hand, press up. I continued to climb, slowly, and so much more tired than the first half of the wall. At least now I was tied to something. I kept moving upward. One step, one movement at a time. I got about halfway to the top when I stopped for a moment to catch my breath. "Is something wrong?" Mikka yelled up as he noticed the rope was not moving for a bit.

"No, just needed a moment before I continued," I shouted back down to him. I started to grab onto the next handhold I could find when the rock shifted again, and it started to tumble down towards the ground. I could see it hitting the earth below and watching it crumble. Knowing that would happen to me if I fell. I looked up and the part of the rock that slipped away created a great handhold in the surface. I reached up to grab onto it, shifted my weight into my right foot, and pressed myself up to grab the handhold. My grip slipped and I started to fall. My left hand slipped off the wall, leaving me to free fall. I heard the rope snap. Then everything went black.

8

"E vergreen, Ever, Evergreen." I heard Mikka shouting at me, but I had no idea what happened. My eyes started to blink open and I could see Mikka, a fire roaring in front of me, and that it was apparently nighttime. "Holy crap you scared me. I'm glad you're awake. I got us some dinner, here sit up and have some food. I have never seen anything like that, you know, what you did back there."

What the heck was he talking about? I didn't remember a thing. It felt like everything was so loud. I blinked my eyes a few times to make sure that I wasn't dreaming. I looked back up at Mikka. "What do you mean what I did back there?" I tried to sit up, but my head was pounding, and I felt exhausted. "You're kidding right? You don't remember? Damn. Ok, well you fell that's what happened. Your weight with the backpack must have been too much for the rope and it completely snapped."

"Yea I remember that part, but everything after that is blank," I said. Mikka looked at me with shock and surprise. His facial expression made me nervous, like he was scared to share what happened. "Well, you fell and almost hit the ground, but then you didn't. It was like your body stopped falling in mid-air, and you... how do I say this without sounding crazy, 'floated' to the top?" Mikka looked down at the ground saying this as if he wasn't even sure his eyes told him the truth of what happened.

"What the heck do you mean I floated to the top? How does one "float" to the top without possessing the power to do so? I was also unconscious. I could not have done that!" I said. I had only ever heard of two Potens that possessed the power to will oneself to "float or fly", but they were old Potens, with years of training, and the natural born skill to do so. "You did knock a tree down the other day, maybe you have more abilities then you were told?" he said. This was impossible. I always sucked at everything. Literally the only gifts I could manage were healing and some small technical ability to will things, and some minor warding. I started to panic. "Did you see anyone else around after the climb?" I started looking frantically around. If I didn't have the power to do this, someone must have been following us. Mikka looked around quickly but shook his head. "No who the heck else would be out here? We're literally so far from everyone, and there is nothing out here."

I started to sit up fast but quickly laid back down, my body felt so strange. I felt like I was experiencing my body from outside of it for a moment. I was extremely dizzy. I knew It couldn't have been me that did this, but who would be following me, wanting me to live?

I didn't have the energy to sit up let alone look for someone and I had no one left in my life that even cared. Mikka interrupted my thought, "after you "floated" to the top, I climbed up as fast as I could, and once I got to the top you looked like you were sleeping." The shocked expression on my face must have startled Mikka because he took a small step back.

"You climbed to the top without the secured rope? That was so stupid! You could have died, and I would have not known what happened or what happened to you!" I shouted.

The anger and confusion raged inside of me. I felt like I was about to be sick. My head started to spin. What in the heavens was going on here? Mikka grabbed food and brought it over to me. "Well, I figured if I didn't get up there, I wouldn't have known what happened to you so you'll just have to get over it. Here eat this." Mikka handed me a stick with cooked meat on it. "Eat." He looked at me and pointed to the food. I was grateful for food and a fire. I felt like my body had been hit by a train. I slowly started to push myself up.

"Thanks, for everything. Seriously. You could have left and taken all my stuff. I probably would have," I said. Mikka laughed. He seemed happy that I was back to my regular self. With a smirk on his face, he replied, "I thought about it, but we made a deal. I don't break deals. And no problem, just eat, have some water, you'll need your strength. If we're sticking to the plan, we need to be up as the sun rises to get to Sutton. We're going to take the train." He sounded certain, assertive, like he was sure that we would be doing that. I wasn't used to that at all – being told what to do.

Mikka looked at me as if he was waiting for me to protest, but I didn't see another option. The train was the fastest way, but it was definitely the easiest way to get caught. We would have to buy tickets, the trains were run by Potens which allowed them to monitor if everyone on the train had a ticket or not. This would mean one of us would have to show our face at the counter which is a huge risk of getting caught. I started to sit up and took a big bite of the food. Nothing has ever happened like this before, what the heck was going on? I needed to get my strength back so we could leave, but I wanted to know more about what just happened. Someone had to be following us. I looked around but was still so dizzy. I laid my head back down on the forest floor. I needed to shut my eyes for a little while.

I must have fell back asleep, because Mikka woke me up with more food. Mikka must have also put me in my sleeping bag, and there was a balled-up jacket under my head. "Time to get up, you've slept for two hours, and we need to get going, how are you feeling?" he said. I felt really grateful Mikka was there, but I was so skeptical of what had happened that I felt like I wanted to distance myself a bit. He could be a Potens and I just didn't know it. You couldn't tell the difference between a human and a Potens unless they showed their gift.

"I am feeling a bit better. I think after eating some more, I'll be fine." Truth was I still felt super dizzy, but we didn't have time to wait for me to feel better. We were on a strict deadline and had to get going if we were going to make it to Halvar in time to meet my friends. "Ok great, I packed up everything so we're ready to go once you put the sleeping bag away." I started to move out of the bag, rolled it up, placed it in the small bag it came in, and put it in my pack. I ate a little more food and gulped down some water. As I started to stand up, my legs felt so funny. I just felt really weak, like whatever happened took a lot of energy out of me.

"You ok?" Mikka shouted over as he started to put his pack on. "Yep, just getting my balance back. We don't have more time to rest, so I'll just have to adjust as we go." I finished packing up my stuff and took a brief look around. I still felt like we were being followed. I kept turning around as we walked away, constantly looking through the trees to see if I could see someone, anyone. "Onward," Mikka said as we started our trek farther into the Sunken Forest towards Sutton.

We walked for miles. My legs were starting to feel better. As far as I could tell there was still no one in sight, although this did not stop me from turning around every few minutes to see if someone was there. Anxiety crept back in as I kept thinking about how I was able to survive that fall. I tried to keep pushing it down, to deal with it later, but it kept rising back to the front of my mind. I tried to think about what we would do next to distract me.

At this rate we should reach Sutton by late tonight, which would be perfect because the train got in every morning at 5 am. This meant it would still be dark so we could sneak onto the cargo car without buying tickets to avoid being noticed. It was the perfect plan.

After walking for 8 hours, the sun was starting to set, and the edge of Sutton was in sight. We could see a road ahead, which was much different than the unpaved forest trails we've been taking. "There, Sutton." I pointed towards the edge of the road to the 'Welcome to Sutton' sign. On the other side of the street there was a small A-frame inn, but the downtown was still about a mile down the road. "We must find camp before we get close enough to Sutton. If we time it right, we may be able to hitch a ride on the train without anyone noticing. Let's setup camp here," I said. Mikka looked at me and then at the small inn. "Why don't we just spend the night there? I doubt we're number one on the wanted list..." He had a point, so many Potens and humans in connection with Potens had been arrested lately or charged with felonies for a list of different things that it seemed unlikely that anyone would truly notice us.

Either way, it still seemed too risky. "I don't think that is a great idea, I just have a weird feeling about it." There was a strong feeling in my gut that we needed to sleep in the tent tonight, after that weird occurrence in the woods, something just felt off.

Mikka rolled his eyes. "Ok, fine, but do you mind if we both sleep in the tent then? It would look less suspicious then if someone came across me sleeping outside a perfectly good tent." I felt sick to my stomach as in the tent with him I had no barrier of protection. I knew I did sleep outside with him last night and nothing happened. Hopefully if he was planning on killing me, he would have done so by now. This was going to be awkward, I mean he is *alright*, but I just met this guy and still was not sure if I can fully trust him.

My grandfather always told me *"everyone has a motive for whatever they do, and they don't always share the truth behind it."* He put his trust in the wrong people and look what ended up happening to him. Mikka was right though, it would look really suspicious if someone were to come by and he wasn't in the tent. Plus, I didn't think my wards were actually working to protect us from being seen. Mikka finding me proved that.

"Yea, sure, but don't make it weird," I said as I looked away. Mikka saw I was holding my axe close because he burst into laughter. "Be quiet," I whispered to him. We still didn't know who owned that Inn and couldn't risk getting caught. There was smoke coming from the small chimney on the outside of the inn. It looked just big enough to maybe have two rooms on the inside. The curtain inside the window of the Inn moved as if someone had looked out right as they heard Mikka laugh. We both ducked under the bush to hide. Once the curtain went back to covering the window, we started to walk slightly farther back into the forest to find a spot to setup our campsite that would be hidden from the road.

We found a spot that looked somewhat hidden from view and started to quietly setup our camp. I pitched the tent. Mikka tried to help but it's *my* tent, and I want to do it my way. I set up my tent in silence, trying not to let any leaves crackle too loudly under my feet. I still had a strange feeling about what happened on the wall. Something about it still felt really off to me. Mikka started to get out some of the food and water. We wouldn't be able to have a fire, the risk of being seen was too high. We both ate some food in silence. Mikka was staring at me as he ate. What on earth was he staring at. "Could you not stare right at me?" I whispered loudly. Mikka let out a quiet laugh and rolled his eyes. I went back to eating my food and ignoring him. I realized that he was probably also in awe that I floated to the top of the ridge. He probably thought I have all of these incredible gifts, but I didn't. I know that there must have been someone following us, watching our every move.

Mikka whispered into the silence between us. "We should go to sleep, we have to get up early to head over to the station." He immediately started quietly putting the stuff back in his pack. We both got into the tent and I crawled into my sleeping bag. Mikka got under his blankets and I turned to face away from him. I tried to ignore how awkward it was to have a stranger sleep in my tent. I clutched my axe as I slept. Mikka fell asleep almost instantly because I could hear him loudly snoring. I hoped his snoring wasn't too loud to attract people from Sutton.

I always had a hard time falling asleep, but after a long while I finally shut my eyes while clutching the axe handle and drifted into dreams.

When I woke up, Mikka was gone. I grabbed my axe to open the tent and found the tent to be at the edge of a cliff. There was a waterfall gracefully pouring over the cliff. The sky was bright orange. I looked over the edge to see where the bottom was, but it was just empty, the waterfall was falling into nothing. When I turned around the tent was gone. 'What the...' My voice trailed off as a loud scream of a woman shrieked in the distance, the entire forest around me started to collapse and the edge of the cliff face started to crumble. I held onto the edge with all my grip, my axe looked like it started to glow. The light from the axe was blinding and my grip started to loosen. The ground I was on fell off of from the cliff into the waterfall below. I slipped and fell into the world of nothing below. "Ever, ever, EVER!" I awoke to Mikka shaking me. "What the..." I hadn't had this nightmare in so long. I used to have this reoccurring dream when I was younger, but it had been years since I dreamt of that place. "Are you ok? You started shaking," Mikka asked. "Yes, just a bad nightmare." I laid my head back down on the pillow and tried to close my eyes to drift back into a sleep. I was embarrassed that Mikka saw my reaction to my dream and wondered what he thought of it.

I tossed and turned for the rest of the night, but I couldn't sleep no matter how hard I tried. I heard a bird chirping in the distance. I knew it was nearing sunrise and it was time to go. We packed up in silence, securing our possessions into our backpacks. I grabbed my golden axe and placed it on the loop on the side of my pack. We were about ready to go when the door of the inn slammed shut. Had someone seen us packing? I tapped Mikka's arm to get his attention. "What was that?" I whispered to him. We both stared in stillness looking at the Inn, waiting to see if someone would come out. Nothing happened.

We packed the rest of our stuff in complete silence. I don't think I've ever put my tent away that quietly. Instead of walking on the road, we stayed hidden in the trees, using them as cover as we headed toward the train station. We walked slowly to try and make the least noise possible, avoiding stepping on loud things that might crack like twigs or branches that were on the ground. The walk felt like it took forever, but once we saw the train station in the distance I felt like I could breathe again. As we approached the downtown near the train station, we stopped to come up with a plan.

The Sutton train station was small, not many people used this stop on the train. I pulled out my binoculars and looked at the station. There was a small ticketing window and from what we could see there were about ten people waiting to board the train. Some looked like travelers passing through, some were workers headed toward Halvar.

"Do we risk trying to get a ticket?" I said as I looked back at Mikka. It was a big risk, but if we boarded without one and were caught on board with no papers by the Potens, we would be jailed immediately, or worse. I did not want to think about what could be worse. "I think it's the best choice, I think I should get the tickets though. Who knows if my crimes were reported yet? They probably think I'm still with the top Hunters or are on the look out for me in the forest north of Kinver. They wouldn't think I'd be taking a train right toward them," he replied.

He had a point. We knew that what I had been accused of was news to everyone near here. Probably because I was just a healer and it was newsworthy that I could have harmed someone. Especially since I had traveled through here before to pick up supplies for my shop, someone would be bound to recognize me. We decided it would be best for Mikka to get tickets instead of sneaking on to prevent getting caught mid-ride, at least here we could escape back into the woods and take the longer route.

I reached in my bag to grab something to give to Mikka. "Ok, you can go but take this with you." I handed him a small greenish-blue pill filled with cream-colored powder. "What is this?" he asked. "See that teacup?" I placed the binoculars on Mikka's face and pointed at the ticketing counter. There was a woman at the counter selling tickets and drinking hot tea.

The glass between her had a large enough gap to stick your hand through. "Once you're over there and after you've purchased the tickets, slip this into her cup of tea. Do what you can to distract her, and make sure she drinks this in her tea. Mikka looked at me and stepped back. "Is this going to kill her?" he said in a low voice, probably second-guessing that I might have murdered that human.

"No... I don't kill people Mikka, despite what some may say. It's a forgetful-draught. I used to give them to people who experience trauma because you can forget what happened in the last 24 hours. It only lasts a few days. She'll eventually regain her memory of what happened. It could be a big help to us right now. She will forget she ever saw you for a few days." Mikka looked shocked. It seemed like he did not know much about healing teas or what they could do. "Uh...ok so all I do is put it in her drink?" Mikka took the pill and held it in his hand for a moment. "Yes, just slip it into her drink and it will do the rest," I said as he put the pill into his pocket. Mikka brushed the dirt off of his clothes to try and look at least somewhat presentable. He still looked like he lived out in the woods, but we didn't have other clothing options. He left most of his stuff with me and grabbed his wallet to head over to buy the tickets.

"Wait here." He turned his head back to look at me as he walked out of the forest and onto the road. I watched him through the binoculars as he approached the station and headed towards the ticketing counter. I looked around through the binoculars to see if there were any train officers nearby, or any of the Kingsmen. There was nothing but what looked to be people and it's really hard to tell if someone is a Potens or not, especially from this far away so I *couldn't* be sure that anyone had any gifts. I turned the binoculars back to Mikka at the ticketing counter, it looked like he was *flirting* with the woman. I rolled my eyes.

I guess that was one way to get the tickets, I mean he was handsome. Not that I really have thought about it. But looking at the way the lady was looking at him through the window, I could tell she thought so. The lady in the window handed Mikka two tickets and he slipped her something under the window. It looked like a small piece of paper. What on earth was he doing? I could see that she was laughing and smiling, and definitely flirting back with him. She turned around in the booth and walked away from the window and as she turned away, Mikka squeezed his hand under the glass and slipped the pill into her tea. She came back over to the window and handed him another piece of paper, this one was golden. He laughed and smiled and started heading to the benches at the station. Time to move. I looked in my backpack for my dusty blue bandana I knew had to be somewhere, and I placed it around my nose and mouth to cover my face. It wasn't unusual to cover your mouth on transportation because of some of the diseases that were spreading like wildfire lately so this would be the perfect way to cover who I was. I put our packs together and started to walk over to the station.

I sat down on the bench next to Mikka and tried to look like I did not know him. "Well?" I said without looking at him, I didn't want the two of us to look suspicious or draw attention. "I've got the tickets, *and...* we've been upgraded to first class sleeping quarters." I tried not to look over to him in shock, but what was he thinking. We were for sure going to get caught in the front of the train. "That is a terrible idea, everyone who rides in first class is usually friends with the King, if not royalty of some sort themselves," I said shocked and upset. I knew in my gut we were going to be caught. My heart started racing.

He kept looking straight ahead with a smile on his face. "Did you not hear what I said? First class *sleeping quarters.* I told her I was transporting my sick sister to Halvar, and she needed to rest as we are on our way to the hospital. I assured her that it would be better for the train and the passengers if we were in a more excluded part of the train to allow you to rest, and not get everyone sick." Mikka stopped dead sentence as another passenger walked by. Once the passenger was far enough out of ear shot, he continued, "We get on, head right to the sleeping quarters, and see no one. We get food, drinks, and are able to stack our packs with anything they have up there. Right before Halvar, we both head to the back of the train and hop off before they get to the station. It's a perfect plan."

This actually was not that bad of an idea. If we got off the train where all the other commoners are, we wouldn't be questioned. However, if we got off from the first-class cart, they would want to see our luggage and to privately drive us to the next location. He slid the golden piece of paper I saw the ticket woman give to him on the bench over to me. It was a First-Class ticket. I read the ticket aloud in a whisper, "First Class Sleeping Quarters – two people – room 15A – Sutton to Halvar." I can't believe he thought of this. This really might just work. "You can think outside the box, I'll give you that," I said still facing forward as I smirked under my bandana. I noticed he also was crumpling a piece of paper and putting it in his pocket, but I didn't have time to ask questions right now.

The roar of the incoming train could be heard from the station. The horn sounded loudly as the train started to approach the platform. The train came to a halt and the doors slid open. A few passengers exited the train in Sutton. We boarded, handed our ticket to the conductor and he instructed us as to which way to go. I pretended to be sick, faking a cough and leaning on Mikka to maintain the story he had told the ticket window lady. As we stepped onto the train, the conductor hurried us along to where we needed to go, fearful that we would get others sick. We headed towards the front of the train, past the business class car, past the bar car, past the kitchen, all the way to the front. I had never ridden on a train before, never had a need to. Kinver was always my home and I did not have anywhere to go past Sutton. This was what being rich must have felt like.

We arrived at the sleeping quarters, found the door to 15A and quickly went inside. There were bunk beds with gold trim on the walls. There was a small chair and a little desk with a lamp on it that had a basket of delicious exotic fruits and specialty chocolate. There were tin water bottles filled with clean drinking water next to the basket. The amount of detail and gold trim everywhere made me feel sick. What kind of wasteful people actually purchase these tickets? I looked back at Mikka. "How did you afford these tickets?" I said with such confusion. "I may have offered that girl a date..." OH. So, he bribed the girl to upgrade us with a sad story and a promise of a date. Solid. Well, it worked, and we were here. I rolled my eyes.

He pulled that crumpled-up paper out of his pocket and on it was the girls phone number. She won't even remember their conversation for a few days so at least she won't remember that she was stood up. "Well thanks I guess," I said as I looked around the sleeping quarters. He shrugged and locked the door to the compartment we were in. Mikka started to grab some of the fruits and chocolates and shove them into his backpack. He looked up at me and made a face, probably because I was staring. "What? We might be hungry later!" he said. He was probably right. He put the tin bottles in our bags since we might need them. We both shared a pinkish fruit that tasted like a mix between mangos and pineapple, and we picked our bunk beds. I picked the one with the window. I started to look out the window and saw there were a few of the Kings Guard walking into the station.

"Mikka look." He climbed onto my bed for a moment to look out the window. We watched as they approached the ticket counter. The Kings Guard had a flyer of some sort in their hands. They were showing it to the lady at the ticket counter and she was shaking her head no. It looked like they were looking for someone. They turned around and started to walk towards the train, but the train's whistle blew, and we started moving. My heart was racing through my chest. "What do you think they were looking for?" I said to Mikka. "I don't know, but I am glad that we won't be finding out." He went back to his bunk and we both laid down for the ride to Halvar.

9

I must have dozed off for a bit because I woke and Mikka was brewing hot tea. Strange that Mikka would brew tea for a *tea-maker*. The gesture was nice either way. I got out of the bed, rubbed my eyes to wake myself up, and let out a yawn. "Whearewearewnow?" Mikka looked at me with a strange expression. "What was that?" He laughed. "Where are we now?" I said back, annoyed.

He looked at me with a grin and I looked out the window, this was no time for flirting. He had done enough of that today with the lady at the ticket counter. "We just left the station in Commauge, we're about two more stops from Halvar. We should start to head to the back of the train so we can make our departure early. I originally was thinking about just walking straight to the back of the train, but while you were asleep there were guards patrolling up and down asking for people's papers, I watched them through our cabin window. I had a feeling it was related to those Kings Guards we saw at the station. I don't think it's safe to just go through the train, the risk is too high. My identification card did not match up with the name I gave for our tickets which would cause questioning. We will have to find another way," he said.

We were trapped on this moving train. My head started pounding. We were so close to meeting my friends I could not have this end here. "There isn't another way Mikka, where else would you like us to go." Mikka had a grin on his face as if he knew something I didn't. As his grin widened, he looked up to the ceiling. There was a small latch that opened from the inside to the top of the train. This could not possibly be his solution.

"No... you've got to be kidding me." This was my first time on a train, but I didn't think we would literally be *on it*. "There's no way that is going to work." I felt cold and started to sweat, each moment of these last few days brought more and more danger. My anxiety was starting to come back. My hands felt clammy.

Mikka stirred the honey and sweets into the tea and handed me a cup. He took a sip of his tea in the other mug in the room. "I worked up a plan while you were sleeping, and I think it may just work. I've been on trains before, and even on top of them. Once we reach the next station, it should take about fifteen minutes to get from there to the station right before Halvar. If we can make it to the back by then, we will just have enough time to climb the ladder down the last cart and head into the woods right before the train comes into the station in Lintown."

I had to admit it was a smart plan, but I had never walked on top of a moving object at high speed and couldn't imagine it would be easy. I felt nauseous, but jumping off a moving train felt safer than trying to outsmart the train guards. Especially when our paperwork does not add up. "Ok genius but how are we going to stay on top of the train? It's going pretty damn fast Mikka..."

I took a sip of the tea and looked out the window to watch the trees pass by at ridiculous speeds. It was difficult to make out what the trees even looked like at this speed. Mikka was looking up at the latch, "We tie ourselves together, I go first, and this way if one of us falls, at least we are able to stop the person from falling." That sounded stupid, and unsafe, and my gut told me no. What other choice do we have though? "I already packed our backpacks up, so we're all ready to go," he said. I looked over at our neatly packed stuff. THIS STATION IS TRENTON. The loudspeaker rang throughout the train. "Ok, we will go, but under one condition." "What's that?" Mikka said as he stared back at me. "Promise to *Never* make tea for me again, this is terrible." I put the tea down on the counter and Mikka laughed. "Ok c'mon it couldn't be that bad." Based on the look on my face he knew I wasn't joking.

The train slowed and finally stopped. I heard the doors open as passengers got off, and new ones got on. YOU ARE NOW LEAVING TRENTON – THE NEXT STATION IS LINTOWN. The loudspeaker rang. This was our only shot. Mikka stood on the small chair and reached up to unhinge the latch on the ceiling. He opened it and I could see the clouds starting to quickly pass us by. He started to pull himself up with the rope attached to his waist. I handed him up the backpacks and then reached up for his hands to help pull me up. He was much taller and made this look much easier than it was for me. Once we were both on top of the train, we kneeled down as he tied the rope to my waist. We both put our backpacks on and Mikka stood up with such ease. I realized that if he fell, I would too. Considering I was so much smaller than him there was no way I could hold him up, but it could be helpful if I were the one to fall. Either way, the rope idea was starting to make me nervous. I came to the realization that it was, in fact, a terrible idea. There was no time to change plans, no time to waste. We couldn't go back now, and it was hard enough to hear anything on top of the train up here to talk about changing plans.

I started to stand and I felt like I was learning how to walk for the first time. This was terrifying. The speed of the train got faster as we got farther and farther from Trenton. My legs were shaking.

I could camp in the backwoods, climb almost anything, but this, this scared the crap out of me. Mikka shouted because the wind was so loud as the train started to swiftly continue to pick-up speed. "ARE YOU READY?" He mouthed. I nodded back. There was no time to scream into the loud noise around us. I had to take this one-step-at-a-time. Mikka started to move forward, the track was fairly straight so it wasn't as bad as I thought it would be. Right foot, left foot, pause. Right foot, left foot pause. I could get the hang of this. My nervousness started to drain away with each step we took.

We got to the second cart and there was a gap between the two. "WERE GOING TO HAVE TO JUMP IT. I'M GOING TO LOOSEN THE ROPE A BIT," Mikka yelled. My anxiety came right back. My heart started to pound out of my chest. Mikka started to put some slack into the frayed rope so I wouldn't fall immediately if he jumped. He looked back at me, and then leaped onto the next train cart. He landed safely, he made it look easy. He signaled me to make the jump next. "Ok Ever you've got this," I whispered myself words of encouragement knowing it was too loud for him to hear me.

I took two steps back and got a running start and leaped. I fell to my knees once I reached the other side, but I did it. I felt the adrenaline running through my veins. "GOOD JOB, BUT WE HAVE TO PICK UP THE PACE," Mikka shouted towards me even though it was almost impossible to hear him. He tightened the rope and we continued onward. We continued this pattern and rhythm for the next eleven carts until we got to the last one. Once we were on the last cart, Mikka took the rope off of himself, and I untied it from my waist, and threw the ball of rope into my pack. There was a beautiful, big station ahead that was just coming into view. As the train approached, it began to slow. It was going much slower than before which made me feel more comfortable making the jump.

Mikka started to climb down the side ladder that was on the left side of the moving train. The train was continuing to slow down as it approached the station, getting ready to come to a full stop. He jumped and rolled off the train, definitely not gracefully, but it did not look as bad as I thought. I headed down the ladder next and although I was absolutely terrified, I jumped and rolled into the bushes. I scraped my arms on the twigs on the ground, but I was alive.

I was several feet away from Mikka since I jumped later than him, but by the time I was about to get back on my feet, Mikka reached out a hand to help me up. "Thanks." I brushed the dirt off my pants and we both looked into the distance at the next station. It looked much bigger than the one we had come from, and more polished. I didn't know much about Lintown, I had never been this far outside of Kinver before. I knew Lintown was for the rich, but it was very small. For the town only holding 2,000 of the elite, the train station looked like it could hold 30,000 people.

"We head north for about thirty miles and then we should be at the edge of Halvar. We could pass through Lintown if we needed to make it shorter." I nodded. It was safer to make the trek from here by foot. Halvar was a huge town and the station there would be impossible to exit the train there without being caught. "Ready?" Mikka said. "Ready," I replied.

10

We headed into the edge of the forest for coverage. As we walked step after step towards Lintown I had a lot of unanswered questions about Mikka and his family. Why would the King take or need his family, why not just kill them on the spot? What did the King need from Mikka? All these questions made my head hurt, but I didn't think Mikka knew the King's motives.

I started to see the edge of the small town. We headed deeper into the forest by the West end of Lintown to enter from a small alleyway between two store fronts. I was about to step out of the forest and into the opening between the alley and the forest when Mikka quickly stopped me. He put his hand on my shoulder to stop me from moving any further.

"Something's not right," Mikka whispered as he signaled me to duck beneath the bushes. "We're almost at Lintown and can you hear that?" he whispered. I tried to listen but heard nothing. "I don't hear anything," I whispered back. "That's my point. If we're almost at Lintown how come we can't hear a carriage, a person, any noise whatsoever of the town," Mikka said. He had a point, it was a deafening silence. I peeked above the bushes to see if there was any movement between the alley way on the street, all I could see was what looked like newspapers covering the streets, blowing in the wind. It truly did look abandoned. "What do we do?" Mikka looked around, and then looked back at me.

"I'm going to go in to check it out, if I'm not back in 15 minutes – head on to Halvar without me. If something goes wrong, don't come looking for me," Mikka whispered. I responded, "No that's insane, you don't even have any gifts, what would you do if you got caught?" Mikka looked annoyed, but he knew I was right. "Fine, but if things do go wrong, we head back here and come up with a new game plan." We nodded and in silence headed into the alley.

We both started to walk forward as quietly as possible. There were newspapers and wanted signs were all over the place - some were of criminals I had heard of some and others looked like very average people, all Potens. I stepped on a crinkled newspaper and slowly reached down to pick it up. The headline read: "POTENS ARE POISONING OUR LIFE AS WE KNOW IT." Underneath the bold headline was a picture the King and a line of Potens in what looked like metal handcuffs of some sort. Under the picture was the article.

"*Potens everywhere have been working in secret to put an end to all human life. They believe they are the higher power, the better race, and we must put an end to them immediately. Every Potens has been sharing the results of their efforts, encouraging each other to work towards ending all human life. If your neighbor is a Potens, they are after you. They are coming for you. We must stop this now! There have now been 302 cases of Potens killing humans in the past 100 days. King Jett issued a royal decree that anyone who finds or knows of a Potens, must turn them in immediately for questioning!*"

What in the *heavens* did I just read? Tears started to well up in my eyes. Not only was this incredibly untrue, but I would have been one of those people accused of killing a human. I looked at the paper as if it was a joke, there couldn't be a royal decree to kill all Potens.

Kinver was fine a few days ago and no one acted weird at the station in Sutton. I turned to see Mikka reading the same article in a newspaper he picked up. He looked right at me and put one finger to his mouth to tell me to shush. He started to slowly walk to the edge of the alley, I followed closely.

As we both stepped out into the street, all the storefronts looked as if they were broken into. There was shattered glass everywhere on the streets, some of the shops were burned, and there was ash all over the ground. Smears of red lined the cobblestones. I knew what that was probably, but would not allow that thought to stay in my mind. I put one hand over my mouth to stop from screaming. How did this happen? "Mikka," I whispered as I pulled his hand. "Where did the people get off at the train station in Lintown?" We realized they were all gone which meant there had to be guards here, picking through the crowds, one-by-one taking the Potens with them.

He looked at me as we both darted into the broken window of the nearest empty storefront. We tried to avoid stepping on any shattered glass, and we hid behind the counter in the shop. As we ducked behind the counter of the small broken shop our eyes were glued to the front of the store. We heard people walking on the cobblestone not too far away. I peered over the top of the counter to watch them when they walked past the store. The footsteps got closer, and they were right outside the door, walking past.

I could hear them talking, but I couldn't make out what they were saying. My heart raced as the footsteps traveled past the store, and I felt relief as they got farther and farther away. I turned around to rest my back against the counter and slammed my hand to my mouth and let out an audible gasp. I could not believe what was lying next to me, two dead Potens. I could see that they were trying to defend themselves when they died.

I started to feel incredibly sick, turned my head and threw up. Mikka reached over to grab my hand. He mouthed, "We need to move" to me and before I could protest, we started to crawl to the front of the store as quietly as possible. I couldn't tell how far away those people that passed in front of the store were, but we had to move now before we got caught.

I cut my knee on broken glass as we made our way all the way back to what used to be the door of the shop. My knee was bleeding all over the floor. I didn't have time to complain, we had to keep going. We got to the edge of the shop and stood up. We tried to use what was left of the building to shield us from the outside. Once we were able to check if anyone was coming, we quietly darted out and headed back to where we had come from. Mikka and I silently went back into the alley and all the way back into the edge of the forest.

I fell to my bloodied knees and wept. Mikka placed his hand on my back, and I could feel his tears dripping onto my shirt. Once I was able to talk, I turned to Mikka and said, "What happened?" Mikka pulled out the newspaper from his pants, and as he read, he looked more and more concerned. "This was out two days ago. It looks like an extermination plan to get people to turn on one another. It was a bloodbath. Lintown was always known for being more *human-elitist*, but I didn't think it could ever get this far... do you think the people in Kinver would riot?" he said with concern. I had thought that the Potens of Lintown were well respected, but it looked like the humans chose to act against them. I wondered where the humans of Lintown were now.

Kinver was more Potens-friendly than Lintown. About half the people living there were Potens. I thought about what the people of Kinver would do. All my customers had been loyal and also had been my friends, so they would have never turned on me...right? I had no choice to let go of what I just saw and put it into the back of my mind. I had to keep going.

The King

King Jett paced around his chambers. He had been pacing for hours now, waiting for his spy to return. There was a knock at the door. "Come in."

The large door squeaked open and in came the hooded man. "What on earth took you so long. I need the answers and you have kept me waiting for hours. As King, I do not wait for anyone," the King said sternly as he stood looking out the window away from the Castle. He was angry and also concerned, since from the time when he became King, everything he wanted seemed to be always just out of reach.

The hooded figure walked closer. "My sincerest apologies sir, I could not leave without being discovered, so I had to wait for the right moment. I do not have the answers you seek, but I did find out that she has family. A girl, just 20. Her name is Evergreen. I sent guards to collect her, but it seems she has run away from Kinver. We will find her sir. We can use her as leverage," he said.

The King slowly pivoted around to see his spy. "Very good. Yes, find the girl. Bring her here alive. Maybe she could be of great use to us." The spy nodded and swiftly exited back through the castle halls.

12

I paced in circles as I tried to come up with a new plan. Why would King Jett issue a decree to kill all Potens? It didn't make any sense. I knew that he didn't like Potens, and that there were mysterious deaths and people being constantly accused, but it had not been this bad.

I turned toward Mikka to get more answers. "Why did everything seem fine when we were on the train? There were several Potens on there, and no one made me suspect anything was out of the ordinary?" I looked at Mikka. "Maybe Lintown was more receptive to the idea. Maybe the idea to exterminate the Potens got pushback and people thought like we did, that it wasn't that serious anywhere else," Mikka said in reply.

He looked down as he tried to put the pieces together of what we had just witnessed. There must have been so much death there, so much. I wondered what happened to all the Potens that were on the train, were they all gone now? There has to be an explanation for it. This could not have happened in just a day. His original campaign was to make this country stronger than it ever was – what happened now? Had he changed his mind?

The idea of extermination would not unite us, it would divide us, making our kingdom much weaker in the end. As I paced in circles, Mikka pulled out a paper map that he had found in the shop that we hid in. He was studying it, trying to find a way to get to Halvar that would be unseen. We needed a new plan, and we needed one fast.

"Ever - what if we went through the Chero trail that leads just outside Halvar? We'd have tree coverage, be off the main roads, and it is more of a direct route than if we doubled back and tried to go a different way." Mikka was staring down at the map. The Chero trail was a well-known hiking trail that people would backpack on normally, but it might be empty now with all that's going on. "Hmm. I don't love that idea, but I don't see a better option. My fear is what if they have hunters waiting in the forest for Potens? I'm not nearly powerful enough to fend off hunters with my gifts alone," I replied. Mikka looked at me with disappointment then looked back down to study his map. "You have a point," Mikka said. He went back to studying the map, trying to find a new solution. That's when it all clicked.

"I've got it. Ever, we could head north into this area...," Mikka's voice trailed off as he pointed down onto the map. Just above Lintown there was a forest that opened up into the backcountry, just west of the Chero Trail. My eyes widened as I realized where he was referring to. "You do realize what you're suggesting here right?" Mikka made a face but he did understand. I felt the blood rush out of my hands and feet towards my heart. What he was suggesting could actually kill us.

Mikka could see that I was visibly anxious and tried to calm me down. "I know, the Zirkel's aren't the safest area on the map, but I don't see a safer route. Plus – with it being well known for *what it is*, there won't be any patrols because who would think to even go there." He did have a point. I've only heard such terrible stories associated with the Zirkel's – mainly the scary stories that were told around campfires for years and years. The Zirkel's were always known to be cursed. An area that few people came out of alive or with their sanity. Not much is known about them, other than what is told by those who have claimed to have been there themselves. The idea of having to head right into an area that had a terrible reputation sent a shiver down my spine, but what other choice would we have? I felt like this entire trip had been one bad decision after another.

I paced back and forth for a few moments, trying to come up with another solution but kept coming back to this ridiculous one. "I can't believe I am going to agree with this, but anything is better than the way Lintown ended up and I think it's the only option we've got. I know that area won't be safe, but we will at least have a chance there rather than heading into slaughter. But after this, if we make it through, please stop suggesting things that might cause our imminent death." Mikka nodded. There was no smirk, no laugh. Where we were going would be incredibly dangerous.

That was that and we had decided on a trek through the Zirkel's. What a stupid idea, but the only option. We both had a snack and refilled up our waters and then started to head out.

I wasn't much for superstition, my life had been incredibly difficult with so much loss so early that I never felt worried because what else did I have to lose? A few *ghost stories* about the Zirkel's were not going to stop me from trying to find out more about what was really going on here – and this being the only option, I would get to the bottom of this if it meant taking a little risk, even if my heart rate was skyrocketing.

We traveled west for a bit before heading north into the unknown of the Zirkel's. Our walk was mostly silent. We continued like this for hours. I kept thinking about what we had seen back there – the destruction of property and senseless killing of Potens in that town. The two bodies I saw in the shop. They probably had families. They probably had dreams. I couldn't get the picture out of my head.

I had seen terrible things happen before, but not of this magnitude. I felt uneasy about my future, I knew there would be no more tea shop – ever. I knew that I would be running until who knows when. The nerves had overtaken me. I had stopped for a moment to grab hold of a tree. I felt like I was going to be sick. The weight in my chest got heavy, it felt like someone was crushing me from the inside, my surroundings started to spin. My breath started getting heavy. I was having a full-blown panic attack. "Mikka," I whispered as I fell over. I laid on the ground as the world spun around me and Mikka came into my view. "Evergreen you are ok. We're ok, we are going to be ok." He put his hand on my shoulder as I spun. I put my hands on my heart and tried to breathe in and out. I tried to slow my breathing, to ground myself into the space I was in. Mikka continued to try and calm me down. After ten minutes, I felt things start to go back to normal. I felt the ground again, the sky slowly stopped spinning and I was able to catch my breath again.

"You ok?" Mikka asked as I sat up and pulled myself to my feet with his hand. "Yea I think so," I said, unsure, but there was no other choice but to keep going. I had lost everything already, my family, my shop, and now it felt like I was to have no future. I couldn't get lost in this thought pattern now, I had to move forward. I dusted myself off, forced those thoughts to the back of my mind for now and started to move forward. I couldn't let that happen again. I used to have panic attacks often, but now was not the time for this. Every minute mattered to distance ourselves as far away from Lintown as we could. Anxiety was something I had struggled with, but I could not let it get in my way right now.

After walking for two hours, we stopped to grab some stuff out of our packs. We both needed to grab water and snacks to refuel. I desperately needed to eat something after puking my entire days' worth of food up in that store and having a massive panic attack. I felt drained. We had a variety of good snacks that we took from the train. We barely said anything to one another, we tried to eat as quickly as we could.

Once we felt ready to go, I looked at Mikka as he started to put his pack on. He was really caring, he could have left me on the ground when I had my panic attack. I am sure he knows we probably wouldn't see my friends in time now and I wouldn't be able to get him the help he needed.

I looked at his eyes. His crystal-blue colored eyes. I knew that he was incredibly kind. I hadn't even known this human a few days ago, but there was just something about him that remained so mysterious to me. Why would he help me when he had so much left to lose? I was staring I realized, and he looked back up at me with those water-colored eyes. "Everything ok?" he said again as he kept his eye-contact with me. "Yes, just thinking about everything, let's head out," I replied as I turned away from his eyes. We headed toward the Zirkel's. After about an hour of walking, we reached the darkened-cursed forest.

Even though I hadn't believed in ghost stories, something about this place was so eerie I felt my gut telling me not to get any closer. A chill travelled down my spine and it felt like the air was thin and cold. The forest looked as if it wanted to speak and tell everyone to go away. It was completely uninviting. As we stepped up to the edge of the forest, I had taken a deep breath. We had both looked into the unknown of the deeply wooded forest, but we couldn't see what was ahead. A thick fog covered the area, so it was difficult to see beyond the first tree line.

The density of the forest made it quite terrifying. But the unknown of heading where the King's Guard could find us felt much scarier than this. I spent so much time alone after I was 15 that exploring unchartered territory felt much less scary than trying to fight the town to keep my house and not get put up for adoption. I had already survived those difficult battles, I could handle a trip through the Zirkels I thought. I grabbed my axe off the side of my pack to carry it instead. I placed it in my hand, it was that soft reminder of a life I once lived, a soft reminder of family. Suddenly I felt all my fear dissipate from my body, I felt like no matter what the outcome, I was ready to try and go into this forest. "Ready?" I whispered to Mikka. Mikka shook his head and onward we went. "Ready," he said in reply back to me. We headed into the dense forest, into the very unknown.

The fog was deep, dark and moist. The cold air made the hair stand up on my arms. The unbearable silence was worse than what we experienced in Lintown as we could hear every little crunch and crack beneath our feet, but nothing else. Each step we took felt loud, it was hard to breathe without the sound of my own breath overwhelming my senses. The stories of this place filled my head as I thought of the monsters that lived within the forest and the hallucinations that drove people mad. I felt those thoughts as if they were on a repeating loop.

Fear started to fill me, but with my axe in hand I kept the courage to move forward. I was never usually the scared type because a little risk and fear usually was something that made me feel alive. But this, this time was so unknown – it felt like true fear, the kind that gives you that extreme discomfort in your stomach that makes you physically sick. It felt like there was a massive weight on my chest again and I felt nauseous again. Before these thoughts could overwhelm me, Mikka stopped in his tracks and grabbed my arm. I looked around, but saw nothing. I could feel the change in his energy, the shift from alert to scared. I slowly, tried not to make any sudden movements and leaned in closer to him. "What is it?" I whispered. He put one finger over his mouth signaling me to be quiet. He then signaled for us to get down low, to make ourselves unseen. We both crouched down to the ground as I tried to listen to whatever it was that was making him so still – making his heartbeat speed up and time slow down.

A slight breeze blew the leaves and they rustled above. That's when I heard it. A howl. A faint, distant howl. I could hear more of them in the distance as we crouched in silence. It sounded like a pack of wolves. All of a sudden, the howls became cries as the animals were being killed. The screams of the wolves were worse than the deafening silence. I slammed my eyes shut as the noise was painful to listen to and wanted so badly to cover my ears, but had to keep listening to see what direction the noise was coming from. I kept imagining the horror that was tearing the wolves apart.

What the heck could kill a pack of wolves? I did not want to find out. We sat like this for several minutes. Mikka signaled to me to get up, so we slowly started to move away from the noise as quietly as possible. We took one step at a time away from the noise. The horrific sounds of the wolves crying had slowly stopped. It had us both extremely alert, a wolf was a predator, and a pack would be difficult to escape. Yet, they seemed to be getting slaughtered which meant whatever was killing them was much worse.

The dense fog made it really hard to know if we were really headed in the right direction or towards danger, but we had no choice. We had to keep going. I reached into the side pocket of my pack where I had hidden my compass, but it was no use – the needle kept changing directions. The area we were in was messing with the magnetic fields. I guess the so-called ghost stories were true. I put the compass back since it was useless here. We continued on for what felt like hours. As far as we could see, the sun was starting to set. Walking, while on high alert, meant that it was crucial not to step on so much as a twig. We were carefully looking around while also looking at the ground below.

As the darkness started to surround us, we slowed our pace. "We should setup camp soon before it gets too hard to see," Mikka said quietly. He was right, this was a dangerous area and setting up camp now might be our best choice for survival. If we kept going in the dark, we'd tire and be in danger for the next predator that came our way.

I started to quietly pitch the tent – we decided Mikka shouldn't leave to get food since I won't be able to see where he went and if the stories of this place were true, then I didn't want to be alone here. We were far enough away from those noises that I felt more comfortable here, but it made me wonder if all the stories were true, if there were other things that could come after us. After the tent was set up, I started to think if there was a ward that I could produce that might deter animals, or worse, from approaching. I started to set the normal wards and then added two more that could completely mask our scent in the tent. I kept wishing that I was better at this because last time they didn't even work. I was interrupted by a loud crackle that rumbled in the distance.

I stood up and grabbed Mikka's hand. The crackling got closer and closer. It sounded like leaves being stepped on. My heart started pounding. I grabbed my axe in my free hand and stood with Mikka, waiting to see what we were going to be up against. Out through the fog came a group of people. There were five of them – they were dressed in raggedy clothing. Mikka let go of my hand and readied his bow and I held up my axe.

13

N o need to be frightened." One of the people who had a large
wooden-made cane spoke out. She had a shaved head with intricate tattoos covering her scalp, a grey robe, and a small bag with
her bow strapped to her back filled with arrows. The second person
was a male, notably tall and with long curly brown hair and a full
beard. He wore a long overcoat with an old bag on his back. He was
carrying a large machete and he kept looking around into the darkness that surrounded us, as if waiting to see if something come out
of the shadows. The other three people stood slightly behind those
two. The woman paused to look at Mikka and I. We stood ready to
defend ourselves.

I quickly took a step back. "Go away! We don't want any trouble,"
I shouted, realizing I may be making too much noise for whatever
else lies in the forest – but I could not worry about that, I had to
focus on one danger at a time.

I thought for a moment about the things I had heard about this
place. Was I hallucinating? I had heard so many stories of people
having gone mad in this forest, but was I imagining this? I gripped
my axe in my hands tightly, so they can see that I was well-armed. I

tried digging my nails into my skin to make sure I wasn't dreaming but I didn't wake up because it was not a dream.

The woman looked directly at me ignoring the axe as if it did not matter. "Is he harming you?" she said. She pointed to Mikka and nodded in his direction. Why on earth would he be harming me? "No. He's *with* me...what do you want from us? We don't have anything to trade, please leave or we will fight." The group of people looked at Mikka and I and nodded. The lady gestured to the male in front and the group started to walk away, except her. The woman moved a step closer. As she moved closer it was clearer to see that she must have been quite old, her skin was wrinkly around her eyes and her hands were also wrinkled and bruised. She continued to step up, one step at a time until she was a shoulder-length away.

She went to put her hand on my shoulder, but I took a step back. She looked disappointed that I wouldn't let her touch me. She looked right into my eyes, like she was looking through my soul and spoke. "You two come with us if you want to live. The Crawlers will be out soon and there will be nothing left of you if you wait for that." She spoke with such conviction. It sent a shiver down my spine, the idea of Crawlers actually being real was disturbing.

Crawlers were what those campfire stories always talked about. All that was known about them was that they were huge creatures, but no one who has seen them has lived to describe what they look like. However, there were plenty of dismembered human and animal remains that the creatures were named Crawlers because the human remains would be found on the outskirts of the forest, as if they were trying to crawl away. The five of them stared and started to walk away.

"Should we go?" I whispered to Mikka. "We don't know if we can trust them," I said. Mikka chimed in. "I don't know if we can either, but if they are right about the Crawlers, I think we should take our chances and go with them. They probably would have killed us already if they wanted to." He was right, they had ample opportunity to sneak up on us, especially in the dark. I did not want to stay one more second in this space if the Crawlers were real. I had wondered if that is what got to the wolves.

Mikka shrugged and we both put the tent away quickly. It wasn't the best job, but we were in a hurry. Once we packed up, we followed the strange group of people into the fog and onward. The four people were too far ahead to see, but the woman was still just insight. We followed her for what felt like a few miles, keeping our distance just to be safe that this wasn't a way for them to attack us and take our things. Funny how I was now with a thief, Mikka, afraid that other people were going to steal from me.

The fog finally started to become less dense and I was able to see an opening ahead. We could now make out the four other people that were just ahead of the woman. The sun had officially set hours ago so it should be darker now but as we got closer there was a large treehouse that appeared in sight, giving off light to everything that surrounded it. I looked at Mikka with surprise and could tell he was just as confused as I was. Where are we? I wondered.

There didn't appear to be any way to get up to the treehouse, but as soon as we got closer, a hanging ladder fell to the ground as if the treehouse was wanting us to head up. The woman with the cane started to climb up the treehouse ladder. She signaled that we follow. The four people, including the tall man, stayed at the bottom of the ladder as we climbed up. I started to climb, and I took a look around. There were several other treehouses – all connected by wooden hanging bridges, all atop the trees.

There were small floating lanterns that all started to light up as the surroundings became pitch black. The hanging bridges that connected all these tiny treehouses together had small fairy-lights that lit the way to guide safe passage from one house to the next. These twinkling lights lined the bridges where you could walk, and they looked like stars. The little treehouses had chimneys with billowing smoke. There were so many more people here, all walking from treehouse to treehouse, bridge by bridge. I could not believe how many people were actually living in this forest. The treehouses were beautifully built. It was magnificent and if I hadn't been so concerned with where we're going, I could have stared in awe for hours.

Once we got into the treehouse itself, I noticed the inside was old, but well cared for. In fact, it was quite homey. The small fireplace was covered in beautiful glowing-stone. The stone itself would have provided enough light to keep the room lit, but the fire was also roaring, making the space warm and toasty. This was welcome since we had been living outside in the forest. The stone of the fireplace glowed a luminescent green and the fire roared orange flames up into the chimney. The warmth of the fire felt incredible after our long trek outside. There were colorful circular pillows set up around the room as seats. I realized my jaw was open when Mikka gently put his hand to my chin to close it. The treehouse village was magical to look at, the amount of time and effort put into this fireplace and the beautiful string of buildings was unbelievable. I wouldn't have believed it if someone told me a place like this existed. I barely even believed the ghost stories about this place, but now I know they were all real.

"Where the *heck* are, we?" I whispered to Mikka. He shrugged. The woman used her cane to help her get down to sit on one of the pillows. She gestured us to sit with her. Mikka softly grabbed my hand and we sat down on the pillows. I moved a little closer to him, knowing he was the only for sure ally that I had at the moment. The woman reached over to a small table to grab a book that was just in arm's length. She looked up at us and then back down at the book. She reached into her chest pocket in her robe and pulled out a writing utensil.

"My knees are not what they used to be. What are your names?"

She looked at us. I looked at Mikka – and then spoke. "My name is Evergreen – Evergreen...RRRRiley, and this is....Mmmili. Mili, yes, um, and we are headed North." I quickly began to get quieter – I hadn't wanted to reveal what we were planning on doing, or where we were headed or what our actual names were. "Mullens is my last name," Mikka added in.

The four people that were with her ascended the ladder and joined us in the circle on circular pillows. The tall one sat closest to the woman. Two of the others had to be brothers. They looked so much alike. They were dark haired, handsome boys. They looked much younger than the woman, but very serious. I'd have to guess that they were somewhere near my age. The last one was another woman, small, curly haired, and her eyes – they were brown, but they almost looked like they had a hint of red. It was beautiful. I could not stop staring as she sat down on the other side of Mikka. It was hard to take my eyes off of hers.

"Why North? The only thing North is Halvar and unless you were planning your own funeral, I doubt that is where you intended to go." She immediately started writing something down. I tried to think of a good lie – I had never been great at lying, but now was the time to come up with something good – as I thought Mikka spoke. "OH. Halvar is North? We must be very lost. Um, we were actually looking for Lintown and somehow ended up in the Zirkel's." Not a bad lie, but she definitely saw right through it.

"Who are you anyways? The least you can do is give us some information on what this place is," I interrupted. I thought it would be the best way to hide my lie from her and the group – to start asking questions.

The few of them looked at each other and back around the woman in the center. "This place – it's called the Mantle." The tall man interrupted her. "Do you really intend on telling them everything? We can't trust them," he said. He looked like he was genuinely worried and annoyed, but she seemed very calm, like she somehow knew she would be interrupted.

"Yes, Alco, I intend to show them some trust so they will start telling us their truth. Considering what they have been saying up until this point were half-truths." She looked at me up and down with a face of disgust that she knew I had lied, but how? She continued to speak, "This place, the Mantle was built back when Potens were enslaved and it was a place of refuge, years and years ago. Not many humans would willingly come into the Zirkel's with knowledge of the Crawlers and other creatures that live here so it always seemed like a good spot to hide. It connects a little over a dozen tree houses. There are only about 40 of us here now, all of us moved up here when the new King came into power. I'm Dova, I grew up in Gerontic, way down south in the Kingdom of Summus Waves... Where I lived in between is no matter, but I've been up here for a few years." She then pointed to the tall man. "This is Alco." She then gestured to the brothers. "These two are Bondi and Gregorio. And this, this is Helena. When the new King took his place on the throne, more and more Potens have been drawn out into the Zirkel's. Unfortunately, not many make it this far..." She looked down at her book and started writing again, as if something came up that she could not forget. She kept looking out the window, constantly looking at something, but when I peeked out from where I sat there was nothing there to even look at.

"Why wait it out here? Why not fight back? We have gifts that humans don't including the King...What is the benefit of waiting here?" I said. I had never even thought about fighting back until meeting Mikka, but he sparked something in me that flamed that desire to overcome the people that suppress us. I turned to look at Mikka and he looked frightened. I totally forgot he was human for a second. I squeezed his hand tighter so he would know I did not mean him. He squeezed my hand back letting me know he was alright.

"Why not attack while there are forty of you? That is enough to try fight the King. You could just fight the ones trying to divide us, the one's who only talk about our differences," I said. Dova looked at me with an eyeroll. "Girl, listen, you have no idea what is really going on here if you think it's just a human vs. Potens issue. It is so much more than that. Forty of us would not even be enough to make it through the castle walls to fight. King Jett has tried for years to convince people like us that he would never spark this divide. That he could make this country stronger, but he cannot. He has been plotting this from the beginning. A divided country is easier for him to control and manipulate the ones he wants to for his own personal gain. Think about what he could gain by humans hunting Potens? Think about it." I looked at Dova with serious confusion, what was she trying to tell me? I actually had no clue what she meant by this. I felt that dividing the humans and Potens would only create war and destruction, not personal gain. "What do you ..." CRACK.

The external silence turned into screams. Bondi and Gregorio hopped up in unison as if they'd rehearsed it. Helena reached into her pockets and grabbed out two large knives and began spinning them around, waiting for something. Alco helped Dova up and it looked like he shielded her from the door with his body. I ran to the window of the small treehouse to see what was going on outside. A few treehouses away, the tree had completely fallen, ripping the bridge connecting a few of the houses off onto the ground leaving the one treehouse in rubble. The few Potens inside were crushed by the weight of the tree, thankfully for them because seconds later I saw them...Crawlers. The Crawlers started to eat the dead Potens. The Potens blood was seeping into the night – wasted, cut short.

The Crawlers were not something I thought I'd see in my life. They were HUGE, way bigger than elephants. They had several hands with claws. Their black bodies looked almost shiny, and I could not see their eyes from here. Maybe they did not have any? Their mouths stretched from ear to ear with several shiny rows of teeth that glistened when the light from the treehouses reflected onto them.

There were three of them, eating the flesh of the dead Potens. Alco calmly said, "Everyone down the ladder, we can head out into the darkness together, if the rest of the Crawlers all heard that loud noise, we will be safer far away from here." Bondi and Gregorio slid down the ladder with ease, making it look like it was no effort at all.

Mikka grabbed my hand and we headed down the ladder. I turned around to get on the ladder and saw Dova quickly grab something out of the desk as we all started to descend into the forest floor. Bondi, Gregorio and Helena headed towards the Crawlers, but they gestured to us to go into the forest. I realized they would die to keep this place safe. They must have had strong gifts because Bondi was rubbing his hands together, creating energy to use into what seemed like electricity. Gregorio started to shift, just like my friend from home. He turned himself into wind – something I had never seen. It was like he evaporated into the air as he tried to push the Crawlers into the tree line.

Helena's eyes started glowing red and her entire body lit up in this red glow. I wanted to see what was going to happen, but Mikka grabbed my arm to move faster as we ran towards the trees, away from the Mantle. My heart felt heavy for the destruction of this beautiful place.

I heard a Crawler shriek from behind us. The sound of that monster being killed was absolutely frightening and at the same time I felt satisfaction knowing one of them was dead. I could not believe that the Potens were actually fighting them off.

We ran as fast as we could and from behind me, Dova gripped my arm. "I can't come with you. I have to stay and fight and help the others, but here, take this map, I know you're headed to Halvar...but it's all gone..." Her voice trailed off. "I can see glimpses of the future and I knew that was where you intended to go but the King destroyed it, the entire city is gone. This is not how I wanted to tell you, but we have run out of time. You would be gone too if you went there. The only ones that are still there are employed by the King himself. The rest are all gone, every single one of them."

My eyes welled up with tears, my friends, my only friends in the world were gone. I went to speak but nothing came out. Maybe they got away. Maybe they had posed as human for so long that people actually believed them. Maybe they were ok. I felt the anxiety coming up from my stomach and into my chest. Mikka must have sensed it because he grabbed my hand to try and stop me from having another panic attack.

Dova turned to the both of us. "This map will show you exactly where you need to go, the answer is a door on the map. Follow that, get the answers you need, and save us all." Her hands shook as she handed me the map, along with something that was wrapped in an old rag. "Take care of each other, no matter what." Her voice trailed off as she ran back toward the Crawlers. Cane and all she ran, going to defend her people from those monsters.

I looked at Mikka with tears in my eyes, I had never seen a creature like that in my life, nor have I ever seen Potens ripped limb from limb. And now I had just heard the worst possible news that anyone I knew and love were killed. Everything, literally everything I had ever known was gone. Adrenaline started to kick in so my panic attack could not. Mikka reached over and wiped the tear off my face and mouthed quietly, "let's go." He gently pulled my hand, and we ran deeper into the forest, completely unsure if we would ever see any of them again. I would never forget the kindness that they showed to us, even if it was only for a short time.

14

We had been running for what felt like a very long time. The sun had risen and set while we moved, it had been hours upon hours. We had to be far from the Crawlers now. We hadn't even stopped to eat or drink – just worked to put space between us and them. It was just us again. Us and the forest.

Out of breath, I turned to Mikka. "Can. We. Stop. For. A. Moment." I tried to get the words out in one sentence, but it was taking so much of my energy. Mikka nodded and we took off our packs and sat down for a moment to catch our breath and get some water. "They might have got out Ever...your friends might have got out before it was too late." He knew that would be all that was on my mind.

"I know. I won't know for sure until we get more answers." I cried as quietly as I could into my hands for a few minutes. I needed a moment to process everything, but we hadn't had time for me to think. My brain started latching onto parts of the conversation with Dova, "*Halvar is gone.*" Kept repeating it over and over. I pulled my hands from my face to wipe my tears and when I looked down at my hands, one of them was bleeding.

I must have held the thing Dova handed me too tightly. I started to open the old rag and inside was a beautiful hand carved golden dagger. It was very similar to my axe. It was jagged and on the handle was an inscription. "Mikka check this out," I said as I moved closer to him so he could see.

"My dove".

"What do you think that could mean?" I looked up at Mikka and his face was so close to mine. He smelled horrible, but so did I. Up close he looked different, so *handsome.* His blue eyes shone brightly as the light that reflected off of the gentle glow of the golden dagger hit his eyes. Mikka wasn't looking at me though, he was staring at the dagger trying to figure out what that meant. "I'm really not sure, but it must have been important for Dova to give it to us," he said. I nodded.

It seemed like it was specifically made for someone that the person must have really cared for. The gold was so similar to my axe I felt somewhere in my gut like my grandfather had made this at some point in time. I wouldn't get the answers I needed right now so I put the dagger in my belt and checked out what else she gave me.

I opened up the slightly blood covered map, trying to wipe some of the blood off. The map was covered in gold flecks that shimmered when my flashlight had hit them. It contained handwritten directions and images on the whole area. "Here," Mikka said as he pointed out the Zirkel's and where we might be right now.

I looked at that space and followed the hand-drawn trail on the map up towards Halvar. It pained me to see the name on the map. Just north of where we were supposed to be. There was what looked like a passageway to get to the base of the Forest of Embers. On the map it showed a square door on the ground just on the outskirts of a lake.

I put my finger on that part of the map and the second I touched it, the path underneath glowed for a moment to show where it ended, right outside the Forest of Embers. I gasped at the beauty of the map. Once I lifted my finger off the map, it went back to normal. "It shows the entrance to be a little north from here, there's a small lake that will be our only way of knowing if we're in the right place."

I turned to Mikka, we were still so physically *close*. Mikka turned his gaze to me, I could feel his breath on my face. He didn't say a word. Just stared into my eyes for a moment. I admired his kindness throughout all of this. I wanted to kiss him. I had nothing left and all that we had been through made me want to reach up and do it, but I did not have the courage right now.

I quickly turned away and said, "Ok, I think we should keep moving until it's light out, I am afraid the Crawlers will follow us." "You're right – onward," Mikka said as he sat up, put his pack on, took another sip of water and started heading toward the lake on the map. We were not sure if this would provide us the answers we needed, especially to help Mikka find his family, but if it got us out of this god-forsaken forest, then it was the right way to go.

We walked all night long in silence, deciding running wouldn't be necessary any longer. The forest opened up to this beautiful lake that danced in the moonlight as the water gently moved from the wind, making the moonlight sparkle over its surface. The shimmer of the moon over the water indicated we were at the right place. It was beautiful, and despite all of the horror that had occurred back there, I allowed myself time to appreciate this moment. After all, all we might ever have is this moment. The sun should be rising soon, but the moon was still awake and bright. I took a deep breath in as I looked at the lake, and then I reached into my pocket to take out the map.

I compared the map to our surroundings to find some reference point. Looking carefully around at the trees, I noticed something that I saw on the map and started to walk in that direction. My voice was low, but I turned to Mikka and pointed at the map. "It looks like the entrance to this 'passage' should be right....over....here." I continued walking to the edge of the lake and saw nothing.

Even with the similarities on the map, I could not find what it was that could have been the door shown on the map. "What are we supposed to be looking for exactly? Is it a door, a tunnel, is there more information?"

Mikka took the map from me to further examine it and I walked around the area where the passage was supposed to start. The sun was starting to come up as the moon's light dimmed and the sun started to shine brightly in the sky. I pulled out the dagger from my waistband. I looked at the inscription, *My dove*. It shimmered as the light crossed its blade when I turned it. I looked up towards the tree line and there – in the leaves of the tree was a single, very small, *golden leaf*. It shone the same as my blade, and I would not have even noticed it if it hadn't reflected the light off of my dagger.

I slowly walked backwards in surprise and bumped right into Mikka who was looking at the map. "Sorry, I just, I, I think I may have found it," I said as I pointed up at the leaf. "Well Damn!" Mikka said in surprise. We both knew that this had to be where the entrance was. It had to be here, why else would have Dova given us the dagger if not to show us how to find the door.

Mikka and I walked all around the tree and there was still no sign of a door, a hatch, nothing. I was looking for any sort of handle, lock, or anything that I could push on to open the door, wherever it was, but there was nothing.

Mikka walked around the other side of the tree. I started to knock on the tree. "What are you doing?" Mikka looked at me with a smirk as if what I was doing was ridiculous. I rolled my eyes as I made a face at him. "Trying to see if it's hollow, you know maybe we have to pull a lever or something I don't know – why aren't *you* helping?" I said.

Mikka grabbed my hand and pulled me around to the other side of the tree. "Because I already found it." He brushed aside the fallen leaves, and there was what looked like a trap door. It was not in the same spot as the one on the map and I wondered if that was to keep it safe and harder to find for anyone who might find the map.

I reached for the murky handle on the top of the door and it creaked. It was a little stuck at first, so I put both hands on the handle and pulled using my entire body weight and the door snapped open, almost causing me to fall over. The handle was rusted over and I got rust all over my hands. I brushed it off onto my pants and looked down the hole that was below the door. "Mikka, I don't think anyone's used this for a while. Hand me your flashlight." Mikka handed over his bigger flashlight and I flashed the light into the darkness of the tunnel.

There was a really old hanging ladder, very similar to the one we had just climbed at the Mantle, except this one looked much older and much less safe. "I'm going to go down and see what it looks like," I said to Mikka. I had felt anxious about what would be below, but what could be worse than what we had just come from. "I could go first if you wanted," he said.

"No, that is sweet of you, but I think its best if I go first, especially since the people at the Mantle were not so fond of humans, I'd rather take my chances in case someone actually is down there." Mikka nodded in agreement.

I descended using the hanging rope ladder into the darkness below. A few of the steps were cracked and as I put my right foot on the next step it completely fell away making a loud thud at the bottom. My heart raced, but I held tightly onto the rope for dear life. I stood there, both slightly swinging and frozen for a moment, waiting to get my balance back.

"You ok?" Mikka said, his voice echoing down into the darkness. I replied, "Yes, but this ladder needs some adjusting, I'm fine." I continued descending very carefully, one step at a time, and after a while, I finally reached the bottom. It was much further to the bottom than I expected, and I was glad I realized that now, rather than when I almost fell off the ladder - otherwise I would have. There were cobwebs everywhere, it felt a little damp, and all I could see was just pure darkness from there on out, making me conclude that it was a long way to the end of the tunnel.

I looked down at the dagger that I had put in my pocket wondering why Dova gave it to us - we already had enough weapons. Besides, nothing would be useful against the group of the Kings men, especially since it was just the two of us. I couldn't see very far even with the flashlight, so I headed back to the end of the rope ladder. "Come on down!" I shouted up to Mikka. It felt like it was a safe bet to head down here now. Anything had to be better than the Crawlers finding us again – I'd take the unknown any day over seeing those things again.

Mikka shouted down towards me. "Ok, I'm going to throw your pack down, get ready in 3, 2, 1..." The pack fell and made a loud thud as it hit the earth and it echoed through the dark tunnel. We had to be far enough from the Crawlers now so the noise should not matter. I grabbed my pack and Mikka started to descend the ladder as he shut the trap door above him. Once he was on the ground, I strapped my axe to the outside of my pack on the side for easy reach if needed, grabbed a little water and looked over at Mikka. "Ready?" Mikka nodded. "Onward," he said.

We headed down into the tunnel. Some parts were so tight it felt claustrophobic. To see, we both put our hands on the walls to guide us forward. It felt moist and grassy. Wet Cobler's Moss covered the walls. Cobler's Moss was something you could chew on to induce sleep. I ripped a little off the wall and put it into my other pocket for safekeeping, could be useful later.

The tunnel got even tighter and we had to walk in a line. The ground was damp with mud, so our shoes got muddy and wet. My shoes felt sticky from each step I took off the muddy ground. I walked into so many cobwebs that I thought I would puke. I *hated* spiders. Even though I loved the outdoors, I could do without those eight-legged bugs.

We continued to trace our hands along the walls to make sure there wasn't another path in the trail along the way. I wanted to stop, the cobwebs made me shiver, but we had nowhere else to go but forward and through them. It was clear that no one had used this tunnel in a long while.

We walked for about two hours and then we saw it – light. "Look." I pointed ahead, there was a glow at the end of the tunnel. Mikka grabbed the back of my backpack. "Ever, you're uh, glow-ing." "I'm what?" I looked down and the dagger in my pocket was ra-diating light and so was my axe. I started to exclaim, "What the..." Mikka looked closer at the axe. "I think it's because we are approach-ing the Forest of Embers and both of these things were made with the same gift." We kept walking and I put the dagger in my hand. It lit up the surroundings, making it much easier for us to continue forward.

I pulled out the map to see what our options were. As we got closer to the end of the dark tunnel, we slowed our pace, careful not to make too much noise as we didn't know what would be at the end. This time there was no hanging ladder, just a door. A really or-dinary wooden door that had cracks in the doorway allowing the light to pour in. I looked down at the map, if this was right, we were right outside the ring of the forest around the castle.

15

I grabbed the door handle and it felt warm to the touch, but something inside me wanted me to open this door so badly. I didn't know why, but I felt like this door was for me. Mikka looked at me and nodded, knowing that we really did run out of options and hopefully Dova was sending us the right way. I started to turn the knob and the light that emitted from the dagger and the axe was completely amplified as the door opened to trees all made of pure gold. It was the most magnificent thing I had ever seen. The gold glowed so purely it was blinding, literally. I had to shut my eyes for a moment to process the vastness of what I was seeing.

Since it was my grandfather who made this I had already heard many stories of this place, but to actually get to see it in person was unlike anything I had ever seen or imagined. The glow of the Forest of Embers was not just from the trees, but it seemed like the birds and any animals or insects in this forest also glowed that golden tone. I did not even know one could will animals to change form like that while still remaining very much alive.

I started to step out of the door to get a better look, but Mikka grabbed my hand. "Ever, we will stand out once we step out of here, the entire forest is one color and we are another, plus we need to come up with a plan. What are we going to do when we get to the castle in Crestwood?" Crestwood was the town where the King resided. The only thing in that town that was active now was the palace.

A long time ago it used to be filled with townspeople and beautiful shops, but when the new king took reign he forced all of those people out of the town and pushed them to live outside of the Forest of Embers so he felt better protected. It has been said that all the old buildings still stand, just empty and ghost-like now, with old memories being the only thing people think about when they see them.

All his lies about creating a connected and joined community quickly came-to-light as he started making these ridiculous royal decrees. The new King promised change, he wanted to create connection between all of the people, but it seemed that the power of his position got to him. The idea of the very empty town sent shivers down my spine. How could someone let that happen?

"Hm, I am not sure what we can do." I let go of the door handle, realizing Mikka was right and we should think about this first. If I opened the door and walked out with no plan, we would be seen. I did want to stand in the forest, my grandfather's creation. My axe always gave me a sense of connection to my family, but here – I could feel whole in some way. I knew Mikka was right though, and we had decided a plan was the best place to start.

Since we were remaining in the tunnel for now, I put my pack down and I opened the door slightly to allow just enough light to get in to illuminate and not blind us. I pulled out the map from my pack and we started to look at it in closer detail. We were at the edge of the map, the passageway door where we were currently located was at the very top left corner of the map, not leaving us much to go on in terms of devising a plan. I had put my hand on the map near the door. I looked back up at Mikka. "Well have you ever been to

Crestwood? What is past this edge of the map?" Little golden flecks on the map shone in the light as the golden glow from outside illuminated the map. "Do you see that?" Mikka was staring in awe down at the map.

Mikka grabbed the map from my hands and walked closer to the door. He held up the map so the light would shine onto the bottom of the map. "What the...." My voice trailed off. The glow from the Forest of Embers revealed an entirely new section of the map that could only be seen when held up closely to the light from the doorway. He moved the map out of the doorlight's way, back into the darkness and the new map was completely hidden. "I have never seen this kind of thing in my life," Mikka uttered as he continued to move the map from the light to the darkness in disbelief. He then kept it steady in the light and I walked over to see what the map showed us.

I realized I was so close to Mikka again - my side was leaning up against his. I looked up at him as he watched the map in awe and then looked back at the map. The gold made his crystal blue eyes sparkle, more than usual. The golden tint that gleamed from outside of the door showed the section of the map that was completely cut off from the other more ordinary part of the map. It was Crestwood. This was beyond unusual because the King did not allow maps of Crestwood to be sold. He didn't want people knowing the layout of the town since he forced all of those people out. In fact, we would be sentenced to death for having a map like this in our possession, but that was the least of our worries right now.

The map showed the Forest of Embers and a river that surrounded Crestwood that flowed from the river north of there. He must have diverted the river to have it intentionally create a mote-like barrier between the forest and the city itself. There was only one bridge over the river which led straight to the gate of the old city. Past the gate lie old apartments, shops, and stores, all abandoned and no longer in use. At the very center of the city was the Castle it-self. The castle icon that was drawn on the map did not show enough detailing to know what the inside looked like, but it was enough to know that, if the images were to scale, it was way bigger than we both had thought. The castle only had one street leading in. There were walls surrounding the castle in the center of the city which meant it would probably be really heavily guarded on that road.

"Do you know where your family is located?" I said to Mikka as I continued to look at the map. "No, but I would think they would be in the prison. My family is human, there would be no need to put them in the Potens-gilded cells." The Potens-gilded cells were small chambers that were rumored to be underneath the castle, well protected and heavily guarded by stone-gifted Potens that had enough gifts to inflict pain on anyone residing in the stone walls. The Potens that created that chamber for the King infused the bars and the walls to weaken anyone in there. It was rumored to be a place of pure torture since you would be in pain the entire time you were locked up. For Potens that were confined for more than a few months, the constant pain got so bad they would plead the King for death rather than wait out their sentence. This was designed so that Potens who were locked up there would lose so much energy in try-ing to preserve their sanity that they wouldn't try to escape or use any of their own gifts. No one knew how the Potens infused their gift into the chamber, or how bad the pain was because most peo-ple didn't make it out of there alive. But from the stories, it sounded like it was enough to drive someone mad.

The prison for human inmates was just north of the castle. There were a few ways to get to that human prison after actually being in-side the city walls. The prison would be the only unsuspicious place to visit since it was the only place in the city that actually allowed visitors. The biggest problem we had is that we were both wanted.

Mikka would be top of the list by now, if they had found out what he had done.

"Ok, well getting in the prison should be no problem, but how do we get through this forest undetected and how would we then get into the city's walls?" I looked up at Mikka as he continued to hold the map up to the light to see the hidden map beneath.

The map shimmered. We could see a blue-tinted path that went through the Forest of Embers. "What is this?" I pointed out the tinted pathway that was labeled as 'Kingsway', but I had never heard of it. Mikka replied, "I'm not sure, but it's worth a try. From what I've heard this forest was not only golden, but enchanted with spells that in some way cause confusion resulting in people's possessions to go missing. My fear is that we try and go through this and it completely makes us get off track..."

Mikka was right, my grandfather was a powerful Potens and heavens knows how he bewitched the gold in here. "We can try and take the Kingsway, since it isn't golden on the map. Maybe it's not enchanted or messed with in anyway?" Mikka said, eagerly looking for other options. Anything at this point was worth the try. I chimed in with another concern, "Ok, but what do we do *when* we reach the gate of the city? We can't tell them were trying to visit your family, they will instantly know it is you."

Mikka looked confused for a moment and then he smirked. What a handsome smile he had, his ocean-blue eyes shimmered even more with the golden tint coming through the crack in the door. I blushed and looked away for a moment. I wish I could get the courage to kiss him already. I had never trusted someone like this, and without having a family of my own, it felt like the first person I could talk to, like truly talk to. I shook the thought out of my head. "What are you thinking?" I spoke out loud, interrupting the thoughts I had about kissing him.

"I had a human buddy named Liam a long time ago, and he is in that prison. We could say we're his family visiting him. He has a sister and a brother so it would be perfect." He seemed to always have some sort of solution.

"Although I like where your head is at, we look literally nothing alike." I knew having a backstory would be important in getting into the prison, but we needed a solid one if it would actually work. "Well, I could be Liam's brother Ryon and you could be my wife." That might just work. Only one problem. "What if they know what we look like? You know, since we are both wanted for murder."

Mikka looked puzzled for a moment. "Well, we could cut your hair. The last time they saw me I was clean shaven and now I have a beard – I don't think they would recognize that." I hated the thought of cutting my hair, but he was right.

"Ok, now *this* sounds like a plan that might just work." The only potential issue would be if they had our pictures to compare us to, but I could not think of anything better, so we had to go with this.

I grabbed the golden dagger. I put my hair in a ponytail. My hair was waist-length. It was always waist-length. The idea of having to cut it short when I had never had it short was frightening, but this meant life or death. I held the dagger up to my ponytail and cut half of it off. I pulled the ponytail out of my hair and my hair sat shoulder-length. "Looks good Ever," Mikka said. I hated how his compliment made me feel. The butterflies in my stomach made me feel sick. I pushed it aside and smiled back and got back to work.

We spent the next hour planning our story to make sure we had all the answers to any questions that might be asked along the way. Such as why we weren't arriving in a visitor's carriage and why we hadn't visited Liam sooner? How we met? How long have we been married? What our home looked like? Where do we live? And any intricate details that might be asked. We had to be super detailed because without any paperwork, we would have to be convincing. Convincing as in, *flawless*.

"Ok, lets head out. What do we do if we get caught?" I said to Mikka as my voice trailed off and I began to worry. I never had much of a gift. I was always the weakest one in my class. But I would be brave today, for Mikka, for his family, and for all of the Potens that have been killed. Mikka walked over to me and put his hand on my cheek. My body heated up as if he had a gift himself. I tried to calm my heart rate down, so that he wouldn't see that I was flushed, but it was too late, he could see. "There is no room for what if's right now Ever, but if you do not want to take the risk, I would not blame you. You've helped me get this far. I am so grateful for all that you have done for me." I wanted to help him, regardless of the outcome.

He brushed my shorter hair out of my face and put it behind my ear. My heart rate only sped up. I felt those butterflies in my stomach again. How could I not help him? I have nothing left to lose.

He moved his hand away and turned away to start to put together his pack. "No, I'm coming with you. There is nothing left for me and you have showed me such kindness that it is my turn to repay you. Also, we're *married* remember, I have to come with," I said with a smirk and an attitude. I tried to make a joke of the situation to distract myself from how I was feeling. I felt nervous about heading into a place that would for sure be my death – but we'd had done this together the last few times and we've made it this far. I had nothing left at home, I didn't even know if I'd ever have a home again.

If this plan was going to work, we had to be convincing together. Mikka smirked back, packed up my pack for me and hid the axe where you couldn't see the glow. I continued to get ready for our journey and wondered what he was thinking. I put the dagger in my belt loop under my clothes to also prevent the glow from being seen and we cracked open the door to the golden forest and headed west toward the Kingsway road to the castle.

16

As I stepped into the forest, I felt overwhelmed that this was made by my family. Everything around me glowed. It was magnificent to see. There wasn't enough time to look at everything though, we had to find the Kingsway before anything happened to us in the Forest.

The path to the Kingsway was not an easy one to find. The forest glowed so brightly it actually had made it hard to see where we were going. We knew the general direction of where we needed to go, but we hoped we were actually headed in that direction. After all it was really hard to continue to check the map if we were in the right direction. The brightness that surrounded us did make it easy to see if anyone else was here, and thankfully, there was no one. We did not want to risk taking the map out every few moments so we kept it tucked away and headed straight in one direction.

As we walked, I took it all in. My grandfather created this. Being in this forest felt so weird to me, knowing that it connected me to my family a little bit more than I ever had been in years. It was truly so beautiful, but also terrifying at the same time. How could one possess the power needed to achieve this type of gold? I resented him for showing people what he could do because it is what ended up getting him killed. The idea that one Potens had the gift to make this really worried me about what else other Potens could do and what the King would do to them if he found that kind of power.

I stared down at my feet to pay attention to where I was walking and to block out some of the blinding light that illuminated everything around us. Mikka put his hand on my shoulder every once in a while, as a subtle reminder that he was there and we both continued onward in what we hoped was the right direction.

The golden leaves that covered the forest floor crackled as we continued to walk forward. The crackling leaves were different than most – it was like they were shattering from being so fragile. It felt bad to be crushing the golden leaves but there was no other option to get to the Kingsway.

The thought that people might come to take some of the gold, even just a leaf, to change their life for the better. The fear of the King's power had stopped people from even wanting to get this close to the Castle or even anywhere near Crestwood. Also the rumors that people lost all of their possessions in here was another reason.

To even take one leaf and risk loss of mind and possessions, stopped me from taking a chance. While these were only rumors, I would not chance it, not when the campfire stories of the Zirkel's turned out to be true. Who is to say any of the stories I heard growing up were fake now. I pushed the thought of taking the gold out of my mind, but it was hard when everything that surrounded us brought me back to that thought.

Mikka grabbed my arm and pulled me behind a tree. He covered his mouth with his pointer finger, signaling me to be quiet. My heart started pounding. I slowly turned my head to peek around the tree to see what was ahead. There were a group of Kingsman. The road was about 40 feet from where we stood. We were so close. My heart started to pound again.

There were six of them, two on foot, two on horses pulling a wooden golden flaked carriage, and the other two riding behind the carriage on horses. This could not be happening now, not when we've almost made it to the Kingsway. They all had what looked like metal masks protecting their faces. I had peeked my head out more to figure out what they were doing when the golden branch of the tree I was leaning on snapped. I thought the gold would make the branch sturdier. I shifted back behind the tree and Mikka's eyes were wide. My heart was pounding so hard, I think the forest could hear my heartbeat in that moment. The Kingsmen must have heard the snap to because the carriage stopped rolling. There was silence for a brief moment.

"Go check that out, we're going to keep on going, were too close and this precious cargo needs to arrive before noon." One of the Kingsmen said to the group. The Kingsmen on horseback and the carriage continued on, but the two on foot headed right for where we were hiding. Their footsteps kept getting closer. I looked at Mikka and a tear streamed down my face. I knew we were going to be found. I reached slowly for the dagger under my belt loop. I gripped it tightly in my hand, knowing that although it glowed, so did everything else where we were hiding. I couldn't bear this being how it ended, not when we were just around the corner from finding Mikka's family.

A deep voice right from behind the tree said, "I can see you, come out now and you won't be harmed." I looked right at Mikka, trying to decide what we should do. He shook his head no. I held out my shiny dagger to see a reflection of what was behind the tree and both of the Kingsmen had their arrows at the ready. They wouldn't keep us alive even if we listened.

They were decked out in armor, shiny gold, unlike what the normal Kingsmen wore. My grandfather probably made it. They were whispering to each other, and I watched them both nod. While I was watching the Kingsmen, Mikka had opened the pack to grab the axe. He had it in his hand and we both stood up with our backs to the large golden tree.

The footsteps got closer. One step at a time they were reducing the space between us and themselves. 'Breathe,' I said to myself internally. Was this to be the moment where my story ends? Would I never recover my reputation and go back to my safe little tea shop? My head felt like it was spinning, but I knew I had to be brave right now. I looked at Mikka and he started to count down. "Three, two, one," he said in a whisper while signaling me to jump.

We jumped out from behind the tree just as they were close enough to touch. The Kingsmen near me released his arrow, but we were so close I was able to push the bow to the side so the arrow shot right past me, just scratching my shoulder, drawing a little blood but nothing time wouldn't heal. He was much bigger than I was, but he didn't expect to miss.

Dagger in hand, I lunged at him, but he grabbed my arm and twisted it backwards. I was stuck. I faced away from him as he twisted my arm to the point where more tears started rolling down my face. I felt the pressure mount and every time I tried to pull away, his grip was tighter, pulling my arm back harder. I was flailing, trying to find some way to escape, but it was no use.

I couldn't even see what was happening to Mikka. I could just hear their fighting and wrestling as they were both on the ground. I continued to struggle to try and free myself, but the Kingsmen grabbed the dagger out of my hand and pulled me closer as he held the golden dagger to my neck. I was not about to just give up. "Who. Are. You. Little. One," he said slightly out of breath trying to keep me contained as I struggled to get free.

"We, we, we, were just headed to visit family, we got scared that you would try to hurt us." The man chuckled. "Absolute, lies. You think I am dumb? Do I look dumb with this dagger on your neck?"

He looked down at the dagger. "With a dagger like this, we will take you straight to the King himself. Must be stolen." We were toast. I knew that this had to be it.

I looked over and Mikka had the other man pinned to the ground he lifted the axe up and he was going to kill him. "I don't think so." The man gripping my body and tightening his hold with the dagger around my neck looked at Mikka. "If you want her to live, you will stop what you are doing," he said. Mikka looked up at me and for once looked absolutely frightened. I tried to whisper 'No' to Mikka, but the knife was digging into my neck, making it impossible to move. Mikka put the axe down and started to stand up with his hands raised. "Good, Soloman, get up." The Kingsmen that was lying on the ground slowly started to get up and picked up my grandfather's axe.

"I'll ask again," the Kingsmen that was holding me said as he started to release me and shoved me toward Mikka. "Who. are. you?" He grabbed his bow and readied the arrow as he pointed it towards me. I looked at Mikka. I was not sure if he wanted to tell them the truth and hope it gave us the opportunity to get to Crestwood or if we should continue to lie. After all, Mikka did kill some Kingsmen, and I do not think they would show us mercy.

The Kingsmen pulled the bow string further back, I started to shut my eyes. The next minute went by slowly. I felt like I was in tune with everything around me. I felt gratitude for the life and the things I had. I could hear my heartbeat and Mikka's. I felt like I could hear the Kingsmen's fingers brushing the bowstring as he pulled it further back and held it in stillness. SNAP. The bow released.

Am I dead? Was this it? The bright glow that surrounded me even with my eyes closed made me feel like I was in heaven. I started to slowly open my eyes and the two Kingsmen were on the ground, both with arrows through them. I looked over to Mikka. He didn't have an arrow. Two thuds sounded behind us and we slowly turned around. Bondi and Gregorio appeared, the brothers from the Zirkel's.

17

I looked at them in amazement. I did not think any of them had survived those Crawlers. I didn't even have time to think about the fact that we almost just died. "How did you....how did you find us? How did you escape the Crawlers?" My voice trailed off. I couldn't imagine what had happened to them back there when we ran. Gregorio glanced over at my backpack.

The top of the rolled-up map was sticking out of the zipper. "The map. We've been studying that map for years and we headed out to find you only shortly after you both left," Gregorio said. "Figured you might need some help," Bondi chimed in. "We knew you two were going to head to the castle - Dova told us exactly where to go," Gregorio said. How did Dova know we would actually take her advice on which path to take – and how did she know we'd be right here in need of help? I knew she mentioned that she could see the future, but I didn't think that she meant that literally.

I was confused, but grateful that they were here. Bondi reached into his backpack and grabbed out a canister of water. He handed it to me. I drank and passed the water over to Mikka. We were both exhausted. Bondi then grabbed something else out of his pack, it was a large tarp. It was shiny and mirrored. "What is that?" I asked Bondi. "It's camouflage. Everything in here is golden, the tarp is a mirror, it reflects everything off itself, so we remain unseen from afar. It doesn't work if people get too close since they would appear in the visible reflection, but from this distance, from the road it will do." Bondi and Gregorio quickly set up the tarp in a tent-like fashion to camo our spot. This was better than my wards that barely worked. Once they were done, they both grabbed hold of the Kingsmen's feet and slid them farther away from the road where they wouldn't be seen.

The sun was already starting to set, and although the sky was getting darker, our surroundings were still illuminated by the golden glow of the forest. It felt like a never-ending night-light of glowing luminescence. The gold at night looked even more incredible then in the daytime. Gregorio decided he would take first watch. He headed out into the glowing darkness with a bow and a pack full of arrows and nodded to Bondi. He climbed up into the golden tree, far enough up where he did not disturb the golden surroundings so to anyone walking by, he would not be seen.

Bondi, Mikka and I headed into the makeshift shelter and sat down to catch our breath. Bondi placed logs in a ring that he pulled from his pack. "Why did you bring those?" I asked Bondi. "We knew you would be in this forest, and you can't make fire with golden logs." Logical explanation, just odd that they knew we would be here. Bondi started to rub his hands together to create that electric shock that we knew he was capable of. It was just enough to create a fire. I was thankful I didn't have to use my sad excuse for a gift to try and light the fire.

The fire crackled slowly. He pulled a pot out of his bag and started to boil some water. I decided I would make us all tea that would give us energy for whatever was to come tomorrow. Mikka had his eyes glued to the map. He was so focused on trying to find us a better way in.

I pulled mugs out of my pack, I only had two, but we could share. I had taken one from the train, never been much of a thief, but I felt like this would not matter. I grabbed my tea leaves and put them on the ground next to me. We all sat waiting for the water to boil. "Bondi, what happened to Dova, Alco and Helena...and well, the rest of them in the forest?" Mikka looked up from the map. He was eager to hear the answer to the question that was just asked. Bondi looked down at the floor, and Mikka and I could see the disappointment and grief in his expression.

He continued to rub his hands together to create that electric shock just enough to stoke the fire, and probably as a much-needed distraction. "We were completely ambushed. We've never had to deal with that many Crawlers, it felt like a set up. I don't know how they all came to our place at once, I mean you *saw* them." He continued to stoke the fire.

He was right, it was said that they did not usually travel in packs, usually they were said to be loners. It was odd to see more than one in any given place. Maybe the stories had been wrong. He paused for a moment to catch his breath, he was filled with raw emotion from the events that must have been horrific. "When Gregorio and I went to fight them, it almost seemed like they were not interested as much in eating us as they were in finding something? It was hard to explain. But I've SEEN Crawlers before, and they don't usually leave bodies with any, and I mean any, meat left on them. These were different. They would bite and kill and eat, but they left the bodies to move forward, almost as if that was not their end game."

"Once I realized they were looking for something, I went looking for Dova knowing she might have the answer. But she was *gone*. Alco didn't make it. His body was lifeless on the ground..." Bondi started to choke up a bit but Mikka interrupted, "Bondi, it's OK, take your time." Bondi took a deep breath and then continued. "We wanted to get Alco's body but there were too many of the Crawlers around. We couldn't risk it. But Dova, she would not have run, she doesn't have it in her to run away – but she was nowhere to be found, not her body, not a trace. Gregorio and I knew the plan if something like this ever were to happen, so we headed out to find you and the map. I was hoping that we would find Dova in the tunnels, but I don't know what happened to her." A tear streamed down Bondi's face and he wiped it away and put his brave face back on. "Dova had told us before you came into the forest, that this was the plan, so I do not know where she had gone." Where could Dova had gone to? I was eager to find out, but I did not want to interrupt him, especially not now.

"When we left, Helena nodded at us to tell us to go. She could hold off the Crawlers if needed. She has *a unique* set of skills, something I have only ever come across once before." I looked at Mikka, and then back at Bondi. "What exactly are her powers?" I spoke out of curiosity from seeing her eyes glow red. "It is kind of hard to explain, you have to really see it to know what I am talking about." He looked back down at the ground. The water in the pot started to boil. He pulled food from his pack. He poured water into my mugs and then dumped the food into the rest of the water. He was making oatmeal porridge for all of us. I asked, "Bondi, what did you mean when you said Dova had this as a plan before we came into the forest?" Bondi looked like he may have said too much because he avoided answering my question. "I just don't know where she went or what could have happened to her," he said in an avoidant reply as if he did not want to share the full extent of the answer.

"Bondi, we'll find Dova. I am so sorry to hear about Alco, but we will find Helena and Dova." I placed one hand on his shoulder, so he knew I meant it. I would help them find their way back to their friends once we finished helping Mikka find his family.

I added the leaves to the tea and willed it all together. The tea turned a lavender color before it turned green. I had lemon shrouds in my bag still. I placed one dried slice in each cup and willed that as part of the tea as well. After a few moments, I smelled the tea to make sure everything was the perfect amount for this energy tea. I craved the perfection of the tea making process. I lifted the tea to my mouth and drank a sip. Immediately, the bags under my eyes disappeared and I had felt completely awake once again.

I handed the tea to Mikka. He too took a sip. He passed the cup to Bondi who was stirring the porridge. He also took a sip. The energy in the shelter felt lighter. Everyone was ready for whatever was to come. The tea was perfection, and exactly what we all needed.

Footsteps jolted me as I heard someone walking towards the tent. I grabbed Mikka's hand tightly. I reached for my axe, but Bondi pushed my hand away.

Bondi just whispered with no fear whatsoever, "Food's ready, we can switch after we eat." Gregorio pulled the tarp aside to come in and sit with us. "How'd you know we weren't just in danger?" I said to Bondi. Bondi looked at Gregorio. "I can feel when its him, it's a brother thing I guess." He shrugged. We didn't have bowls, so we all dug into the food in the pot together. I gave Gregorio some tea. We sat in silence for some time, worried, but hopeful that now that we had Bondi and Gregorio that everything was going to be alright.

18

After we had all finished eating, Bondi headed out to take next watch. Gregorio reached over to where Mikka was sitting, "Can you pass me the map?" Mikka nodded. He handed the map over to Gregorio. We were all so focused on the map - all you could hear was the slight crackling of the dying fire.

"Ahh." Gregorio pushed all the things we had on the ground, backpacks, pots, mugs, out of the way. He was making a space for him to show us the map in more detail. He placed the map flat on the ground and peeled the tarp back so we could see the secret map that lay beneath that became exposed when the light of the gold hit it. The hidden map was beautiful – it was hard to believe someone had the ability to make a map like this.

Gregorio had taken a sip of the energy tea and then started to explain the map. "So, since Crestwood itself only has one entrance, we have to use it to get into the fortress. Once we're in, we can travel east to this alleyway between the city walls." He pointed at a small alley that separated the old business district and the old commoners living spaces. "I've actually been there, a very long time ago it feels like. They used to sell meat pies in that alley, and they were the best in all of Crestwood. I would steal them for Bondi and myself so we wouldn't starve since it was a little more hidden and much easier to escape." His voice trailed off, as if stuck on the sight of a memory. "Gregorio, you were in Crestwood?" I was shocked. It's been years since they've let anyone in without visitation rights to see a prisoner.

"Bondi and I grew up in Crestwood as orphans when the old King was ruling. We know the city pretty well although I am sure a lot has changed. It's been years." He looked back at the map intently.

I was shocked that they could be orphans. How could someone abandon two talented Potens? I didn't want to pry so I changed the subject back to what we needed. "How are we going to get past the gates though? The guards are not going to let us in willingly." Gregorio smiled. He looked like he already had all the answers. "They don't have to let us in. We're walking in with full permission to enter." He peeled back the tarp slightly further to show all the armor from the two dead Kingsmen had been taken off their lifeless bodies and put in two piles right outside the tarp. "We're going to bring you in as prisoners." The idea was way better than what Mikka and I originally had come up with. This would actually get us right up to the prison with weapons in hand.

This actually might work. My only concern is what to do after we got in. Would we be executed? Both dread and hope filled my chest at the same time. I did not want any of this. I so ached for the comfort of my tea shop, for the simple and full life I once had.

I fake smiled up at Gregorio and then looked back down at the floor as I wondered what would come of all of this. Gregorio's smile went from his face. "Well why don't you two get some sleep while we wait for Bondi to come back. Then we can head out before sunrise to go to the Castle gates. While you two are asleep, we will come up with a plan for what happens once we get through," Gregorio said. I knew that each step closer to the Castle and our movements inside would be very risky. I grabbed some of the Cobler's Moss that I pulled off of the tunnel walls earlier out of my pack. I handed some to Mikka and I instructed him to chew on it. It was supposed to help you fall asleep faster. With Bondi and Gregorio here, we needed to get a good nap in before we headed to the Castle.

Gregorio nodded towards the sides of the tent where we could get comfortable enough to take a nap. As much as I wanted to help with the plan, I was so incredibly exhausted. Plus, never having been to Crestwood limited the help I could provide.

There was not a lot of space in the tent-like shelter to get comfortable. Mikka and I slept with our heads almost touching one another. I tried to get as comfortable as I could, knowing that earlier today I almost died and might die tomorrow if we got caught. I closed my eyes and with the help of the Cobler's Moss I fell right asleep.

I awoke and was all alone again surrounded by the forest. The tent was gone, and I was at the edge of a cliff. The waterfall poured over the edge but this time when I looked over, I could see the ground underneath. The waterfall flowed into a river. A girl shrieked loudly in the distance. My heart was pounding in my chest, not this again, please not this. I tried to wake myself up, I knew this was a dream, no, a nightmare. Ever WAKE UP. I screamed, but nothing came out. The cliff began to crumble away, and I tried to run this time, into the woods but I just couldn't run. I slammed my axe into the side of the cliff, praying it would hold my weight. The axe started to glow, brighter and brighter and my hand slipped. I started falling, falling, *falling*.

My body jolted awake and I heard movement right outside the tent. It startled me so much that I sat up too quickly and my head hit the tarp. I forgot we were in such a small space. I must have actually fallen asleep because Mikka had his hand touching my arm. He must have moved closer to me when we slept. Bondi was packing up the food and the brother's stuff on that side of the tent and Gregorio popped his head in. I slowly pushed Mikka's arm off as I blushed since Gregorio had seen. The movement of his arm woke Mikka.

He looked confused, but after a few minutes he was alert. We had been running and on the move for so long, it felt overwhelmingly amazing to get even a few good hours of sleep. Mikka and I gathered our stuff on our side of the tent and started to pack up everything exculding the tarp. When we got outside of the tarp, Bondi and Gregorio were almost fully dressed in the Kingsmen's armor. The only thing missing was their metal face masks which they told us they would put on when we got closer to Crestwood. While the brothers were a little shorter than the two guards, the armor looked very convincing. They wore it well and this actually might work. A glimmer of hope filled my chest, we might have a way in. I had to remember to focus on one step at a time rather than worry about what would happen when or if we actually got past the gate, so I took a deep breath and pushed that hope back down deep inside.

"So, once we get through the gates, I am going to instruct Gregorio to take the two prisoners to the prison cells and I will say loudly that I am going to update the rest of the Kingsmen and the King as to what happened here. I will tell everyone that you two were thieves and that this was all a trick to steal the King's gold on the Kingsway road," Bondi said. Bondi pointed to the map to show us where he would be heading. We would be splitting up at that point.

My heart sunk. Even though I did not know them well, the last thing I would want is for something to happen to them. They saved us after all, and I wanted to make sure it was for a good reason.

"Well then what? What happens when you separate from us?" I said, urgently looking for answers. Bondi looked at Gregorio and nodded. "I will head to the prison where they might be keeping Mikka's family. Once I'm in and pass through the guards station, I'll see if I can free them." He reached into the armor by his waist and pulled out a chain that was connected to a large set of keys. "One of these might be for the prison cells. If this does not work, or they are not there, we will all meet up at the clock tower on the left side of the square by dusk." He pointed right to the center. The height of the tower would give us an advantage in finding a new place to look for them or try to escape back out of there. Although I did not like the idea of separating, this could really work.

We all packed down the tarp and the shelter we made, drank water and ate a few snacks before we decided to head out onto the path. We started walking to the Kingsway path, it was only 40 feet ahead but once we were on it, I felt like our lies would be exposed.

I was nervous that this path would lead us all to our deaths, but there was no time now for another panic attack.

My brain raced with thoughts that we would not be able to actually pull this off without getting caught or made an example of for the rest of the Potens. I was not even skilled enough to be worthy to try and beg for my life in exchange for the use of my gifts because I really was not good enough at anything that would be worth their time. I took a deep breath as I stood at the edge of the path. Mikka grabbed my hand and nodded, "It is going to be ok. We're going to be ok." He reassured me. I nodded back and exhaled after what felt like I was holding the longest breath of my life and stepped out onto the path.

19

As we walked down the path, the golden light of the forest illuminated everything around us – so much so that it was actually quite hard to see where we walked. Mikka and I were both in very loose handcuffs, loose enough that we could slide our hands through when needed, but tight enough to give the illusion that Bondi and Gregorio were actually guards taking us to the prison gates. Bondi and Gregorio finally put their masks on to hide their faces – it made them look fully the part they were playing. This felt like it could really work.

We all walked in almost silence with the exception of the crunch of the golden leaves at our feet. The Kingsway path itself was not golden, but the leaves from the forest were scattered on the dirt path, leaving a trail of golden flecks as we walked.

We did not speak because we were afraid that as we got closer there could be people listening to what we said so we stayed in character. Plus, I think all of us were nervous enough about the potential consequence of being caught, imprisoned and put to death if we were not perfect at our ruse.

The giant castle walls that guarded the old city started to appear in the distance, growing in height with each step we took closer to the gateway. I looked over at Mikka who was in complete awe. It really was quite incredible to look at, especially knowing this was built by humans' years and years ago with no Potens help. But the feeling of dread did not leave me as we moved forward.

As we approached the Castle entrance, we traveled over the moat bridge. The King had designed the moat to surround the Castle as protection. The drop to the water would easily kill anyone who fell in. There were spikes made with wood protruding from the water that would easily impale any that fell, a guaranteed painful death. A chill went down my spine knowing that if we were caught, that could be our fate. I pushed that thought aside, now was not the time for anxious thoughts.

"You two are late...what do we have here...?" The guard at the left of the gate asked with what sounded like a smirk on his face. Gregorio answered "These two..." Gregorio stopped mid-sentence to kick Mikka in the shin. It was quite convincing, even to me. "Thieves...were in the woods waiting for a cart or a carriage to pass to steal from us." Gregorio kicked Mikka again and this time it was hard enough that Mikka fell to his knees. I looked at Mikka with such distress, but I knew we had to make it look as convincing as possible, so I spit in the direction of Gregorio.

Bondi shouted at me. "Do that again and it will be the last breath you take," he said. He spoke it with such conviction that it truly scared me, making this all look very real.

"We heard them in the woods and what took so long was that they tried to resist when we tried to detain them." Gregorio looked at us for a moment. "By the time we could get them to cooperate and tell us about what their plans were, it was dark so we camped until it was light enough to continue, hoping the rest of their group would show up before then." The left guard looked at the right guard. "You were supposed to be at the Kings Quarters at 8AM this morning.

He's not going to be happy that you are both late regardless of the reason." They stared at Gregorio, waiting for a suitable answer.

"Yea well he will understand when we tell him that there are others, friends of theirs that are planning to ambush one of the cargo carts later today." Gregorio pointed at us signaling that we were the ones planning the ambush. The left guard pulled his face covering on his helmet up and had a shocking expression underneath. "Well, that is something isn't it after all. It looks like you found her." He paused while he looked at the right guard. My heart started pounding out of my chest, what did he mean by he found her? I cannot be that high on the wanted list for killing someone by tea.

The right guard nodded. "We can take this lot over to the prisons so you two can catch up with the King's Guard to inform them of this plot." I started to sweat. This was it, we were going to be separated. "Nah I got it. I want the credit for finding her." Gregorio interrupted, making it seem like he knew what the guard was talking about. "I'm taking them to the prison. This one really messed up my left hand and I want to get him back before putting him away if you know what I mean." Bondi kicked Mikka again.

Mikka shouted this time. We had to be convincing enough for them to let us pass without them on our tails. The two guards were smiling at Mikka's present and foretold pain. It made me furious. I wanted to kill them for enjoying this. Bondi looked up. "I'll take the information to the Guard myself. I want to inform them of the plan and where their friends will strike next so they can be ambushed."

The two guards looked at each other and nodded. "Alright, alright, head on through, but hurry up, we don't need any more of the cargo stolen. Not like last time. Plus, the King will want to see her immediately." Gregorio nodded in agreement.

The guard pulled a lever and the gate started to rumble. The sound of the gate opening was almost deafening being this close. The gate fully opened which allowed us all to step onto it. I looked back at the moat and the thought of falling from this height into it made me sick to my stomach. Being in handcuffs made be especially uncomfortable, vulnerable.

Gregorio and Bondi shoved us forward, trying to continue to make it as realistic as possible. The gate was made of pure gold and shone so brightly in the sun it hurt my eyes. It made it hard to keep my eyes opened. We took each step carefully forward, knowing that this path actually might be the stupidest decision we've made but it was too late to turn back now.

What were we thinking? Heading right into the sealed and guarded territory of the only enemy we have all ever known. Once we were all the way behind the castle walls, the Guards closed the gate behind us. The rattling of the gate shutting and locking sent a shiver down my spine. Sealed in, completely – no way out.

Bondi nodded at Gregorio and headed to the right towards the prison in order to see if he could find Mikka's family and free them. Gregorio, Mikka and I were supposed to find another way out knowing that there would be no way to go back the way we came in with the prisoners.

Whether we found Mikka's family or not we would need some sort of an escape plan. Although the gate was heavily guarded, the King would have another escape route in case of an attack. He had become so heavily hated that there is no way that he would not have a backup plan if things went wrong – now it was our turn to find it.

Right before we turned the corner, I looked back at Bondi again. Although we hadn't known each other very long, he saved us and because of this I felt like I owed him everything. Once we were out of sight of the guards, Gregorio released our chains.

"What do you think he meant by found her?" I said. Gregorio looked at me as I asked that question. "I'm not entirely sure but I don't want to wait around to find out. Let's get moving."

I started rubbing my wrists because the weight of the chains was so heavy, they started to hurt my hands. I then looked up at the wall I was standing next to. There was a massive poster. The sight of the poster almost brought me to my knees. "Potens are traitors – Potens are the enemy." The picture was of a Potens strangling a human to death with roots from the ground. The Potens in the picture must be able to manipulate the earth.

It was heartbreaking to look at. The picture showed such force that it would make any human scared to live peacefully alongside us. I felt the weight of the world crushing my chest. Mikka looked at it and shook his head, he grabbed my hand for a moment as the tears started to stream down my face. He could see I was really struggling to understand why this was happening and he pulled me close so he could give me a hug. I could feel his heartbeat this close. The strength of his arms surrounded me, making me feel safer knowing that he would not look at me in that type of way if I was a monster.

I wiped my tears and looked up at him. Our faces were so close now, I could feel his exhale. "Let's get out of here," I whispered and looked over his shoulder at Gregorio and he nodded. Each moment with Mikka felt strange. It was like we had known each other for a lifetime and yet I wanted to know so much more about him. But there was no time for that now. We started on our search to find the backup exit.

Without Bondi, we were more vulnerable. Bondi had the gift of electricity, he could create lightning out of thin air by manipulating the static charges that were already in the environment. I knew Bondi was safe because with that gift he could incapacitate an entire room of people. It still was nerve-wracking being in a protected area, that was specifically intended to keep us out with only one person with a significant gift to protect us. My gift wasn't going to help us at all.

We rounded the corner of one of the buildings and found a small, very tight alleyway. Gregorio pointed and we headed down the alley.

It was exactly like they had described it. I wondered if it was weird for the two of them to be here, in a place they used to call home. Home was a weird word, I hadn't felt at home in a while, even when I was at home.

We kept moving quickly. We couldn't risk taking the map out without fear of someone seeing it – it being a dead giveaway for us being strangers to this place.

The alley was damp. It had moss growing up the side of the brick walls. There were several doors that we passed as we walked through, but they all looked like they hadn't been used in years. Since the King made Crestwood *his,* all of the people who used to live here and create artwork, food, and so many different types of clothing all were forced to leave, pushing them out to Halvar or to the edges of the Sunken Forest.

With the exception of the Castle, a lot of Crestwood was empty from commoners which meant blending in was impossible here considering Mikka and I did not have armor. We would stick out if anyone saw us.

We were nearing the end of the tunnel where we were supposed to come out right in the center of the Crestwood square. From here we would be able to see the clock tower and from there we could find likely places for the backup exit. Gregorio was in front, I was behind him, and Mikka behind me. I reached to tap Gregorio's shoulder "What if he put the emergency exit under the castle?" I whispered to Gregorio. "I don't know, I feel like he wouldn't want to exit through the Potens-prison, because if there was a prison breakout he would have nowhere to go." Mikka nodded. "I think we should try the Court House first, the old Community Meeting Center next, and then under the Castle. My fear is that when we get there it is a trap for anyone who tries to visit." He had a point. The King was smart and did always seem to be two-steps ahead. Gregorio agreed.

Gregorio peered his head out of the alley and then he vanished. "What the...." My voice got quieter. Gregorio manipulated himself into a slight breeze of wind and wisped away for a few moments. Mikka grabbed my hand and we waited. It was weird how calm I felt when Mikka was holding my hand. He had this way of making me feel like I'd be alright.

After what felt like the longest five minutes of my life, Gregorio appeared again in front of us, in human-Potens form. "There are seven guards patrolling the top of the Square – they all are armed with enough arrows to kill 50 of us. The arrows all have golden tips, I have never seen that before, but it looks like they *glow*. The alley next to us leads directly to the Courthouse – we cannot go through the Square without being seen so we might have to retrace our steps and go in one alley over," Gregorio said. "We can't do that," I whispered quite loudly. "We won't have enough daylight to check all three of these places if we go back." I looked around and about fifty feet back in the alley from us was one of those very old, unused, moss covered doors. "What if we went inside – I know it would be a risk, but if it was possible, we might be able to go through this building into the alley next to it. These buildings are old and unused," I said. Gregorio looked around once more, trying to find another option.

"We can try it, if it is no good, we can retrace our steps like Gregorio said," Mikka chimed in. It did not seem like trying to go through this door would be any higher risk than anything else we had done.

"Ok but let me go first." Gregorio insisted he lead since he could evaporate into air if we needed him to take someone down. We all walked over to the door. He tried to open it, but it was locked. It would be too loud to try and break it down.

Mikka tapped Gregorio on the shoulder and reached into his pocket to grab out a small pin. He started to pick the lock and within seconds the door was open. "Where did you learn to do that?"

I was impressed that he had learned this skill, but not surprised considering his family's upbringing.

Gregorio opened the door and slowly walked in. Mikka held the door open for me as I got closer and he leaned in so close to my lips and whispered, "We all have our secrets." He smirked and pulled away to lean his arm out as if pointing for me to go inside. Curious. There was so much I wanted to learn about him.

Gregorio moved so quietly you couldn't even hear his feet touch the ground. I wondered if that was part of his gift or not. Me on the other hand, I felt like every step I took, a different floorboard creaked. I wasn't the most graceful.

Mikka had secured the door behind us, leaving us a way to escape without alarming anyone that we were here. The room we were in looked like an old kitchen and cobwebs lined all the countertops to the handles of the pantries. There was extremely moldy almost unrecognizable animal-chewed food on the counter - probably from when these people got the notice to evacuate for the new King.

Gregorio evaporated into thin air for a moment as he went through the house as a mere breeze. When he returned, he spoke out loud "Clear. There was no one there, completely abandoned. There was a door to the other alleyway on the other side of the house. The only thing is that the Courthouse will be heavily patrolled, and they will definitely notice if we walk right in. I checked to see if a window was open that I could just go through using my gift, but everything is sealed shut." I looked back at Mikka and then again at Gregorio "There has to be another way." I thought for a moment in silence. That was when it hit me. "Wait, are there any pipes? What if you went through the pipes while using your gift, then you could get over there to check if there was a passageway undetected." I couldn't believe that I thought of that, but I think it could actually work.

Gregorio smiled at me. "Not a bad idea Evergreen, not bad at all. Let's check the basement for a clear route." The door for the basement was right next to the kitchen. Next to the door was a long corridor of what looked like it led to a few more bedrooms in the house.

The house was bigger than anything I had ever lived in, and when it was all cleaned up, I was sure it looked beautiful. Right now, it was just a memory for someone, left to collect dust and cobwebs. On the corridor wall was a picture. The picture was of a family of five, happy and smiling. I think it was taken in the courtyard. I looked down to try not to cry, I wondered where they all were now. I also wondered what it would have been like to have a large family, or even a family at all. I pushed these thoughts aside, there were way more important things to worry about right now.

Gregorio opened the basement door and to no surprise the wooden plank stairs were also covered in dust and cobwebs. Mikka started down the stair next, and I continued to follow them. The basement felt damp and cold. I immediately got the chills from how creepy and abandoned it was.

It looked like this family used it for storage only so there was a very strange array of things piled up. There was an old sofa with a stain on it, a broken lamp, boxes of books, canvases that were never touched along with stacks of paint cans, and old shoes. Nothing was organized and it was all just thrown down there in random piles. The three of us started to look around for any type of venting or piping that could lead in the direction of the Courthouse. Mikka started going through the pile of junk to see if there was anything that we might be able to use later. Gregorio was looking in every corner. There was this beautiful necklace hanging off the side of one of the many boxes. It had a thin gold chain with a small symbol hanging off the end of it. I picked up the necklace to see what it was and realized it was a tiny golden dagger symbol with a turquoise handle. It reminded me so much of the dagger Dova gave us. Dova. I couldn't stop thinking about what happened to her.

"This could be useful," Mikka shouted and the sudden outburst frightened me so much that I dropped the necklace. I went to pick it up and realized there was a drainpipe underneath the box. I started pushing the box out of the way to access the opening. "Guys, LOOK!" I shouted. As I turned around, I saw Mikka holding a set of knives. Mikka and Gregorio came right over to see the piping system.

"Great work Ever," Mikka said as he helped me up off of the ground. He handed out a few of the knives to each of us to hide in our outfits for protection. We could use any weapons we could find.

Gregorio put the knives in his belt. "I'm going to eat something and then I'll go, I need my strength if I am going to transform for that long." Gregorio pulled some of the dried fruit slices out of his uniform. We had packed all the essentials in his inside pockets under the uniform. He had the packs still, but in case someone took them we wanted to make sure we were covered with food and the axe, map and dagger.

Using your gift took energy, and if you were to use it for a long period of time, you needed a lot of it. It was vital to make sure you were as close to full energy level as possible. It took time to regain your energy after you used a gift and time was one thing we did not have.

After he quickly refueled, Gregorio was ready to check out the Courthouse. "I should be about ten minutes. If it takes longer than that, go to the Community Center without me. Do not risk waiting for me. I mean it, not a second longer than ten minutes." I looked at Gregorio. "Be careful. Please." I hadn't had family for a long time, but I thought that this is what it would have felt like to have some, to care about others well-being and to have them care about yours.

Gregorio evaporated into a mere breeze, it was an incredible gift to have. You wouldn't even know he was there. He wisped away into the drainpipe and Mikka and I stared at it in silence for a moment until we both decided to sit down and wait for our friend to return.

20

We had been staring at the drainpipe listening for any sound that might come out of it. Anxiety filled the room as we waited. Mikka broke the silence that was so loud it could have been cut with a knife. "You know, I'm really glad I met you. No matter what the outcome ends up being today, I'm happy I got to spend the day with you, even in these circumstances." He looked around at the gross moldy basement we were sitting in. I laughed knowing that it was such a funny thing to say when we were sitting in here. "Well, you know what, me too," I whispered back. I wanted so badly to move closer to him, to show him what I meant and what he meant to me, but the fear of rejection set in and I couldn't bring myself to do it.

Instead, I looked into his eyes for a moment, those beautiful blue eyes, and then looked back at the drainpipe. Mikka had been there for me and I had been there for him this whole time. It felt right to be this close to him. I wish we had more time together, but for now we must find our way out of this castle, hopefully find Mikka's family, and start over somewhere where no one will know who we are. Then I could show my feelings.

We sat in the silence again. I grabbed his hand to hold in anticipation for our friend to get back. I started to feel the sweat drip off of my forehead, I had realized it has been ten minutes. I broke the silence this time. "Hasn't it been longer than ten minutes?" My hands were so clammy I let go of Mikka's and wiped them on my pants. Mikka nodded. "We will wait a few more minutes and then we're going into the Courthouse to see if he is ok, but we are not leaving here without him." The sweat started to drip down my back, something felt really off.

Out of the drainpipe came a wisp of cool wind and Gregorio appeared once again. He was kneeling on the ground, out of breath and his arm is bleeding. "What... what....happened?" I whispered as I looked at him bleeding. His arm was completely cut open, he looked in pain and exhausted.

"We. Have...to. Go...now." Gregorio managed to get out in a very out-of-breath whisper. He got up. We all immediately fell to the ground from the noise that came out of nowhere. *The siren.* The emergency siren was alarmingly loud. "They know we're here. I think Bondi is in trouble, I can feel it." They had said their brotherly connection allowed them to feel if something was off. The idea that Bondi might have been in trouble made me worried, but there was no time for that right now. We had to move. We all got up off the ground and headed up back to the door. We had to go somewhere to try and find an exit.

Panicked, we headed back toward the first alley we went to, with an alarm blaring it was not going to be easy to find a way out, especially with no way to blend in. Gregorio was exhausted from using his gift for so long. Gifts weren't something that could be used continually, it took a lot of effort to do so. Thinking of that, my grandfather must have been exhausted after creating the Forest of Embers, it was so vast. Mikka opened the door and peeked his head out to see if anyone was coming. I grabbed the axe out of the pack and placed it in my hand – gripping it with my life. The dagger went into my belt for easy access, as well as the hidden set of knives I had on me.

Mikka grabbed hold of one of the two swords Gregorio had on his uniform that he stole from the Kingsmen. Gregorio had the other sword in hand – we all knew we didn't have long to get out and we needed to find Bondi.

Once we realized the coast was clear, we headed back down the alley towards where we came from. We needed to trace Bondi's steps. We were going to try and find him first before getting out of here.

It would be impossible to get to the Clock Tower undetected now, so our only hope was finding him and hoping his gift would be enough to help us all. I felt useless, what help was my stupid gift in all of this. We ran quietly but swiftly back to the first turn we made. Mikka looked back just for a moment and then looked at me with a terrified expression on his face. "Run. *Faster,*" he shouted out of breath. We were being chased. There was a group of Kingsmen running this way. They all had their armor on and were heavily armed.

This cannot be the end. Thoughts of my life started to flash before my eyes. I pushed the thoughts away and tried to think of what we could do to escape. I anxiously started to look around for a door, a new alley, anything, but there was nothing.

Gregorio tried to turn around to use his gift, but it completely took the rest of his energy and he collapsed to the ground. I tried to pick him up, to carry him to get out of there, but I couldn't lift him for long. Mikka reached down to try and pick him up and he was able to get him to his feet, but the guards were closing the gap between us.

"You won't make it with me. Go, go without me, find Bondi," Gregorio whispered in pain from exhaustion. "No, we're sticking together no matter what happens, I'm not losing you too." I had lost too much already. I was not going to give up on my friend.

The group of Kingsmen behind us were gaining on us, closing the

healthy gap we had to only 40 feet. We wouldn't be able to run with
Gregorio in this state so Mikka placed him gently on the ground and
we got ready to fight.

I held my axe in hand, ready for anything and Mikka had his
sword drawn, ready to take down whoever came our way. We stood
in front of Gregorio, protecting him from them. "It's too late – we're
too late." Gregorio tugged on my pants as he sat on the floor and
I turned around to see we were completely surrounded. We were
stuck in an alley, completely guarded on both sides.

"Oh. My. God," I whispered as I tried to move to Gregorio's
other side to keep him between both Mikka and I as he regained his
strength. The group of Kingsmen in front of me stood in unison. In
the middle of the crowd of them it looked like someone was coming
to the front. The crowd moved forward in unison, trying to intimi-
date us. It was working.

They all stopped ten feet from us and out of the crowd came Sir
Frieon. He was dragging what looked like a man on the ground. As
he got closer, I realized it was Bondi. My heart sank. His face was
completely black and blue, swollen, and the side of his head was
bleeding. He was beaten really badly. Gregorio screamed loudly at
the sight of his brother in that much pain, it was almost as if the
second he saw him he mirrored that pain.

"Well, what do we have here, a bunch of traitors and wanted
convicts? I'll tell you what, this is a first, the first time we've ever
had people who we were hunting come right to us. Mikka, Mikka
my boy, how good to see you." Frieon stepped closer to Mikka and
ripped the sword out of his hand. He looked at Mikka with a grin
filled with revenge. Mikka had killed Kingsmen, *his Kingsmen*. My
chest filled with pain. I knew there was no way they would let us
live, especially Mikka. Frieon took a step back and then punched
Mikka in the face, knocking him to the ground. I gasped "Don't hurt
him!" Frieon laughed.

With Mikka's sword on the ground, they forced us all to our knees. I slowly knelt down knowing that protesting now wouldn't get us anywhere.

Frieon stepped forward right in front of me. He knelt down to be face to face. He pulled his golden mask up to reveal his face. His armor was different from the others. He had badges and seals of honor melted into his chest armor. He had a scruffy beard and dark brown eyes. He cleared his throat and then said, "Now, listen very carefully, we know that you know where she is. If you tell us, we will let you live. Well, not all of you, we have business with Mikka. But, if you choose not to tell us, and that would be the wrong choice, well let's just say you'll all end up in a landfill somewhere, gasping for your last breath, asking for death."

We all looked at each other, What in the heavens was he talking about? I decided to speak up, but it was so hard to get the words out "Frieon...ehem...*Sir Frieon*, who exactly are you looking for?" He looked at me and started to laugh. All the Kingsmen joined him. It was a noise so terrifying because their laugher echoed off the alley walls. It felt like the entire castle mocked us. Frieon looked at us like we were out of our minds.

"My dear girl, you cannot think I am that stupid, you know exactly who I am looking for and I know she came here with you. Now tell me, WHERE. IS. SHE." In that moment, he kicked Mikka in the face. Mikka's mouth was bleeding, it looked like he might have broke some of his teeth.

I screamed, the sight of Mikka being hurt right in front of my eyes hurt me too. He then kicked him in the ribs continuously as he shouted towards us. "WHERE. IS. DOVA?" I looked over at Gregorio with a puzzled expression. Why would they want Dova? "Please, please," my voice trembled as I spoke through the tears. I wanted to tell them to stop hurting him, that I couldn't see someone else I loved to get hurt. I realized I had loved him, and it was so much more than a physical connection – I mean we hadn't even kissed yet, but I loved him.

"Please stop hurting him. We do not know where Dova is, Mikka and I barely even *know* Dova." Frieon let out a low laugh. "Barely even know Dova? You have to be kidding me girl. How could you expect me not know who your grandmother is? Do you think I am to be a fool? Now tell us where she is now." His smile turned to a serious expression.

What did he mean? My head started to spin. I never heard about my grandma, my parents always told me that I didn't have one and that it was not important, never any story. How could Dova be my grandma? None of this made any sense. Confusion and anxiety started to consume me. My chest filled up with this pressure – my hands started to feel numb. I looked down at my hands, everything was blurry. I looked up and the world around me started to get fuzzy and then everything turned black.

21

I blinked open my eyes to see that I was on a cold wet floor. The last thing I remembered was being outside, trying to protect my friends. I started to sit up. My head was pounding, had I passed out? I started to regain consciousness and noticed the ground was hard, like rock. I started to look around as I continued to blink my eyes and regain my vision. There were bars surrounding me on three sides. I was inside a cage, *a prison*. The one wall behind me was damp cobblestone and there was a constant dripping coming from the ceiling, creating a small puddle on the ground next to me that kept splashing me slightly with every drip. There was a small hole in the floor near the wall, probably what they considered to be a bathroom for the prisoners.

I looked through my cell bars to see where everyone else was. *Mikka.* Mikka was on the floor of the cell in front of my view, passed out and bleeding from the beating he took from Frieon. He must have hurt him worse, after I passed out, because his injuries were very bad.

"Mikka wake up," I started whispering to him. "Mikka please wake up." I did not want it to end like this. I wanted to tell him how

I felt. I moved closer to his cell. "Mikka, I am so sorry." I sobbed into my hands, he was not moving. I hadn't got to tell him how I felt.

"Evergreen." A whisper that came from behind me interrupted my tears. I turned to see both Gregorio and Bondi in one cell on the other side of mine. I felt relief in seeing them. The fact that we were all together gave me slight hope. I slowly stood up to walk over closer to them on the other side of my cell. It felt like it took every ounce of energy to stand, but I was determined so I pushed through.

Gregorio looked much better than before but very weak. Bondi needed medical attention, he looked way worse than Mikka.

"Thank heavens you guys are safe, where are we?" I asked, hoping for them to shed some light on the subject. I continued to look around but moving used up so much energy.

"We're in the Potens-gilded prison, under the castle itself. It's slowly draining us of our energy – slowly taking our gifts and life-force. The walls will consume our energy and our gifts. I'm afraid there is no way out of here," Gregorio said. I felt shattered. This was it. All of this was for nothing. This was the place we had heard about. I started to continue to cry into my hands, I wanted the safety of my tea shop and the simple life I knew before. Crying felt exhausting here trapped in these soul-sucking cells.

I wanted so badly to go back to human activities like climbing and camping for fun. I wanted to make people well again with my teas. Crying made me feel weak. I was not weak – I would not let this break me. I pulled myself together and tried to contain any energy I had left. I realized my pack was gone along with all of my possessions. They must have taken them when they put us in here. I was crushed. My grandfather's axe meant more to me than anything, if I could find a way out of here, I would find a way to get it back.

I grabbed onto the bars of the cell to pull myself up and they felt warm in contrast to the rest of the cell. I wondered if it had something to do with the Potens-gifts that were infused. Curious. I started to look around and there were so many cells all the way to the end of the hallway where I could see a door. I wondered where the otherside of the door let out.

I crawled over to where I could see Mikka. "Mikka I'm sorry. I'm so sorry we couldn't save your family. I am so sorry for all of this," I whispered in his direction, not knowing if his unconscious self could hear. "I don't know if we will make it out of here, but I wanted you to know that I love you. You're the only family I have now." I meant it. I wanted him to know even if it was the last thing I did.

I sat and looked at him for what felt like hours – waiting for him to awake, but he didn't. I kept checking back on Gregorio and Bondi, but Bondi was also in really bad shape. We sat in silence, waiting for someone to come in and tell us what our fate would be. There was no way to escape from here. I looked around for a drain, a window, any type of opening that we could try and find a way through, but there was nothing. I laid my head down. I felt exhausted. I could no longer keep my eyes open anymore and drifted off to sleep.

When I awoke nothing had changed. I didn't know how long I slept, but I had less energy now than I did before I fell asleep. The cell was draining my energy. It made it difficult to sit up, but I did. Everyone was still right where they were. Mikka still hadn't woken up. I wondered how long it has been since we have been in here. Hours or days? The time seemed to feel irrelevant when the energy was slowly draining from my body, minute by minute.

BANG. A loud noise erupted and shook the entire cell block. I couldn't tell if I was dreaming or not, the exhaustion made it hard to tell the difference.

The Potens-gilded iron bars on a few cells down flew open and crashed and crumbled on the ground in front of our cells. It was so strange to see the unbreakable iron dissolve into nothing.

I mustered up the energy to stand, using the bars as support. I wanted to try to see who was coming out of the cell that was just blasted through. My heart felt like it stopped for a moment.

Helena. Gregorio and Bondi gasped in unison as they saw their friend headed this way. How did she find us? How was she doing this to the metal? I thought that Potens could not use their gifts against this.

The Kingsman that was guarding the door at the end of the hall yelled, "STOP. NOW." As he held out his weapon and directed it towards her. He was holding a long stick that had electricity zapping back and forth from the end – a Potens creation for sure, no human could have put that together.

Helena had a hood on, but her eyes glowed that beautiful red that stood out from everything else around them. Hope filled my chest as I watched her. I had never seen anyone else have that kind of gift, that kind of *power*. She slowly turned around towards the guard. She was so small, it was hard to believe she could be a threat to anyone, but judging a book by its cover is always a sure way to get yourself killed. She was someone that people would not expect to be dangerous, tiny and definitely overlooked.

Helena looked at the guard and his facial expression changed from angry to scared. I could see that she curtsied toward him. In just a moment, our fate changed. She then in one swift movement threw her hands in front of her and the guard started to shake and then dropped dead. "What the...." My voice trailed off and I took a step back into the safety of my cell. I had never seen anything like that in my life. Potens were not allowed to use our gifts to harm anyone, but Helena just killed that guard without hesitation. She looked at me and smiled. "Don't worry lady, he's not dead. *Just resting.*"

Her eyes stopped glowing and she looked at Gregorio and Bondi. "Did you think I was just going to let the two of you, inexperienced, *kids* come here alone?" She smirked at them and they smiled back. She grabbed ahold of the bars, as if the gilded cells did not have any effect on her powers and they crumbled into nothing. Gregorio and Bondi were freed, and I could see that they both instantly started to feel better since the cursed Iron was no longer surrounding them on all sides. It looked like Gregorio took a deep full breath in, feeling what it felt like to be normal again.

Bondi's wounds even started to heal up, the cell slowed the healing, even on Potens. Helena then stepped over to my cell and did the same. The second the bars crumbled I felt like I could breathe normally again. Standing didn't feel like such an effort anymore. The effects of the cells was impacting me more than I even knew.

"Thank you." She nodded. She opened Mikka's cell the same, but he was still lying on the floor. I ran to him. "Why isn't he getting better too?" I said to Helena. Helena looked frightened for a moment. "These cells are not supposed to be for humans. Potens have thicker blood than they do, and the impact is probably too much for him to handle. Gregorio, Bondi, we need to carry him out of here." My hope disappeared as quickly as it came back. If Mikka didn't get better soon, I wondered if he would ever recover. The two of them hurried over and each grabbed an arm to put over their shoulders. This was going to be challenging with them trying to carry Mikka when the two of them were not in the best shape right now.

Helena looked around and gestured in one direction out toward where the opening of the cell was. "This way." We all followed her towards the entrance of the prison. There were so many Potens in each cell, I wanted to free them all, but we did not have time. We got to the entrance. The door opened into an alley at the back of the castle. It was a storm cellar. We were about to walk up the stairs when Helena stopped.

She turned around toward the prison for a moment. She pushed her arms out in front of her and all the iron-gilded cells started to crumble. The entire Potens prison was falling apart. "Give them *hell*," she said to the Potens who started to regain their gifts and leave their cells. I felt hope rise within me. This felt like our chance to overcome this madness.

I wanted to get as far away from here as we could. But something felt off. I pulled on Helena's cloak to get her attention to get her to turn around. "Where are all the guards?" Surely in a prison as important as this one, with people they were specifically looking for in it, it would have more guards than just one at the most important cells in the city. Helena looked around frantically, as if she realized we were in much more trouble than we were before. "Hurry, this way." We followed her and as I turned around there were several Potens running in all different directions trying to find their own way out. We couldn't bring them with us right now, it was too great a risk.

Helena started running faster. Although Gregorio and Bondi were pulling Mikka's weight, they started to run as fast as they could in her direction. I looked back at the Potens leaving the prison, beaten and weak, but alive. I hoped they all make it. I turned back toward my friends and ran after them. Helena led us down an alley, this one was at the base of the Castle itself. We ran until we couldn't see the end of either side of the winding, dark alley. We stopped at a manhole in the ground. Gregorio and Bondi put Mikka down for a moment to catch their breath. Mikka was slowly regaining consciousness.

I held his face in my hands as I kneeled beside him. "We're getting out of here, don't worry." He blinked open his eyes at me, he looked terrified. "What about my family? What about Fern and my mom?" I did not have words for him, but he knew. We had to leave now or there would be no one to come back to rescue them. "Please Evergreen, please don't leave them here." The Siren alarmed – we were out of time. "I'm sorry, we will come back," I whispered. I meant it.

"Through here." Helena lifted up the top of the manhole with her gift, I wasn't quite sure what she was gifted with, I had never seen someone with so much power. "Through here there is a network of pipes, we can follow them out to the Moat of the Castle and then get across from the bottom. It is how I got in." She headed down the ladder that was inside the manhole and disappeared into the dark tunnel. From the top viewpoint, the bottom was completely black so all I could see was her descent into the darkness. Gregorio headed down next, then Bondi, dragging Mikka to come with him. Mikka was protesting, he wanted to stay, but there were not enough of us to fight the entire Guard and free his family. We would have to come back. I looked around before I descended and slid the manhole back over to cover our tracks.

It was terrifying, climbing down into the darkness, but one step at a time I continued my way down the ladder. I was so focused on each step of the ladder that when I finally got to the ground I turned around and all of my friends were being held by guards. Each one of them had a knife to their neck, all the knives were golden, just like the dagger Dova gave me.

Frieon pushed through them to step closer to me. "Girl, you cannot think we are that stupid. None of you will be getting out of here alive." I stepped back, into the ladder and Frieon grabbed my arm. "You will all have no choice but to talk now." He turned around and gestured to the King's Guards and they all started walking right down the drainpipes. There were at least 30 Guards down here. Frieon clipped an iron band around my wrist. I looked at my friends and they all had one, all except Mikka. I immediately tried to see how to get it off, but it seemed to have melted together – making the bracelet permanent.

"What. What is this?" I stammered over my words as I asked him to try to slip the bracelet off of my wrist. "Wouldn't you like to know." He laughed as he avoided answering the question. Why didn't Mikka have one? Where was he going to take us? The hope I had before completely disappeared, knowing that after trying to escape there would be no way they would be lenient on us. "Helena use your gift," I whispered to her, this was the time to take them all down. She whispered back "I can't, the bracelet, I think it is draining me of my gifts." I realized that this meant we were imprisoned without a cell, we were all mortals with them on. "I thought that didn't affect you," I said after seeing her destroy the Potens-gilded cells earlier. "This feels different," she whispered. I felt sick to my stomach. This must have been some powerful Potens to have made something that worked against Helena.

We all walked for what felt like a mile. Another ladder to another opening above was mounted on the wall. A group of Kingsmen went first and then we were instructed to go one-by-one up the ladder with Guards in between each of us. I was sure this was the end for us all. I did not understand what they wanted with us or with Dova. I still hadn't wrapped my mind around the fact that she was my grandmother.

As I stepped out of the darkness into the light at the top of the ladder, I saw what I had dreaded all this time. I stepped up into the Square. It was filled with Kingsmen and the King himself was sitting on a golden chair upon what looked like a small stage. The ground was cobblestone, I kept almost tripping as Frieon pushed us all forward toward the stage. I wanted to scream, I wanted to run in the opposite direction. I hadn't wanted any of this to happen, but here we were.

The Square was quiet, deadly quiet. As though everyone knew we would be killed. It looked like most of the Potens that had escaped earlier were in chains, all with the same iron bracelets standing at the side of the stage. Some of them had to have escaped I hoped.

Although the area was filled with people, it felt like everyone was looking right at me. The sound of our footsteps echoed in the silence. There was someone kneeling on the stage, their arms were behind their back, in chains. As we got closer, I could see that it was a little girl.   Next to the King was another individual, sitting in a chair, hood covering their face. I couldn't see who it was, but it must have been someone important enough to sit beside the King. Mikka gasped. "No. no. NO." He started screaming. "Fern. What have they done to you?" The little girl that was bound and kneeling was Mikka's little sister.

Mikka pushed his guard away, headbutted him in the face and started to charge forward with his arms behind his back.

"Mikka stop. Please." I pleaded for him to not try and fight this, we would not win like this. A tear streamed down my face as I tried to beg him to cooperate. Five guards started grabbing him and tried to keep him still. The guard he headbutted walked right up to him. He put his face not even an inch away from Mikka's. He smiled and then lifted his arm and punched Mikka in the face, over, and over, and over, until Mikka was bleeding from his mouth and nose.

"SSTOOP," I cried out as I completely lost my will to stand and started to fall onto the ground. The Kingsmen behind me picked me up and Frieon stepped next to me. "This is not even close to how bad it is going to get Ever." Frieon spit on Mikka while he was down. The anger and disgust in that moment raged in my gut. I wanted to scream. I wanted to fight, but I couldn't move.

They shoved us all forward toward the stage so we would be right in front of the King. All the Kingsguard stepped back so it was just me and my friend's right up front. The King was looking down at a manuscript or something, but then the wind blew, and the top of the page flipped up and I could see that it was the map Dova gave me.

I looked over at Gregorio and Bondi and we all knew that it was our map. I knew what we had done was bad enough, but having that map meant we would be immediately sentenced to death.

The King was still looking down at it when he started to speak. "Well, I made a bet with Frieon that you would walk right into the castle instead of us having to find you and let me tell you I love being right." He smiled while looking down at the map.

King Jett slowly looked up and snapped his fingers so his servants would come over and take the map from him so he could get up. It seemed ridiculous because he could easily have moved the map to the table next to him, but he seemed like he loved having people do things for him - privileged.

The two servants rushed over, both had the same iron bands that were on my arm. They took the map and gave him water and then they rushed back to the sides of the stage. He stood up. He had a solid gold crown and a red velvet suit. He wore golden necklaces, rings, but no diamonds. He looked tired. His scruffy beard complemented his face well, if he wasn't the cruelest person in the world, he would be quite handsome for his age. If he hadn't filled me with rage, I would think he looked quite like a King should look. But in this moment, I wanted him dead.

He stood over us, smirking. "Evergreen I knew you would come here. I knew you wanted to finish what your grandfather started." I looked at him with a puzzled expression on my face. I wanted to explain how I had no clue about any of this, how I did not even know Dova was my grandmother until they told me – I just could not seem to get the words out..."It was only a few months ago that I discovered what he did. You weren't even a blip on my radar then. But when I found out, I knew that he would have given you the answers before I had him killed those years ago. You were the only person left that we could find from your family. I had forgotten that I had your parents killed, what a pity."

He slowly paced the stage back and forth as he spoke. "I didn't even realize something was wrong until someone had brought it to my attention, I thought it was just a string of bad luck – but it seems it was so much more than that."

I looked over at my friends, we were all so confused. King Jett looked at this servant in the wings. The servant rushed over quickly with my axe, MY axe, and handed it to Jett. "Now, tell me, how do I break the curse." I felt absolutely hopeless, I had no idea what curse he was referring too, and I knew his cruelty way too well that I didn't think he was going to believe me. There had to be something I was missing. "King Jett." My voice trembled as I spoke.

"I am unaware of the curse you are talking about, I did not even know that Dova was my grandmother until you had told me, I am a mere tea shop owner. Was, was a mere tea shop owner. I came here to look for Mikka's family, not for the Crown or for Dova. That is the truth sir, you have to believe me." King Jett stepped back looking just as confused as I was. "Ah, I see. Mikka's family. Fern is it? You really think I am to believe that you didn't also know that I needed Fern in all of this as well?" The King laughed as he walked over to Fern and knelt down near her.

Mikka burst out with any energy he had left "DON'T YOU TOUCH HER." The King laughed louder. "You are stupid, despicable mortal. I am not going to hurt her – I need her to achieve something much greater than you two." Mikka struggled to get free but was too weak now.

King Jett got back up and paced for a moment as he was deciding what to do next. I felt like I was not breathing as he paced, my heart was pounding out of my chest, but it felt like I could not get any air. Why would they need Fern? The confusion of it all made me dizzy, maybe it was all a dream. There were too many surprises. Too much to take in.

He came to a stop at once from his pacing. "Well, I guess if none of you can assist me, there is no need for any of you anymore. Guards, take Bondi and Gregorio...separately and bring them to the station, they might be of use later." Two of the Kingsmen behind us grabbed them both and started to pull them away. "As for Mikka and Evergreen, kill them. Oh, and Fern, take her back up to the castle. She doesn't need to be here for this any longer." "NO," I screamed but no one even seemed to react.

This was it for us. The Kingsmen readied their bows on their arrows. Fern was still on the stage, but she was crying, she was so young and scared. A guard was trying to get her up, but she was resisting, she did not want to leave Mikka here. I could not imagine what they would want with her. The Kings man pointing his arrow at me was wearing full armor and a face shield but I could see their eyes and the wrinkled bags around them. Weird that they would be old and in the Kings Guard but that was not important now.

Before they started to countdown, the wrinkly-faced Kings man in front of me winked at me. I did not move, unaware of what might happen if I reacted. I kept my face still, trying to maintain my body language.

Frieon started to countdown. "Three, Two." The wrinkly-faced Kings man turned around and shot two arrows, quicker than ever at both the other armed Kingsmen, dropping them both dead.

M y jaw dropped open as I couldn't begin to understand the nature of what was happening around us. The rogue Kings man
threw a dagger at Helena, but it missed her, only hitting her
bracelet. The bracelet fell to the ground, unhinging Helena from
what bound her gift. "DUCK," the wrinkly-faced Kings man
shouted. Bondi, Gregorio, Mikka and I all laid down on the ground
as arrows swished behind us, all missing the Kings man in front
somehow, like they knew where every arrow would be.

I looked over at Helena who was quickly revived, back to her
powerful self. Helena looked down at her hands and then closed her
red-glowing eyes. She held her hands together like she was trying to
push them into one another. Her body started to move as she closed
her eyes, using all of the power she could muster. All of the Kingsmen in the Square started to shake and they all fell down.

It was a terrifying site to witness, all of their bodies lying on the
earth beneath us. The chained Potens to the side still standing, in
shock of what they were witnessing. I ran over to Frieon to check
his pulse, he was still breathing. It seemed like they all were, just out
cold.

We didn't have that much time to waste. The hooded man in the chair that was next to the King was the only one still upright, unaffected by what Helena had done. I turned to see the wrinkly-faced Kings man standing in front of us, unmasking themselves for all to see. It was Dova.

The King looked infuriated. "Jett, while I must say you look well, your face says otherwise." She was so old, but moved so swiftly with such precision with her bow and knives it was amazing to watch her in-person, my grandmother. She did not even have her cane, I wondered if that was all an act.

She continued to speak. "You must not be that *stupid* to think Evergreen would have any answers for you. You have to see by now that she was not a part of any of mine or Siron's plans." Dova was talking about my grandfather, her lover. It was still all very strange to me.

Dova continued to take her armor off. It made me nervous, she was exposing herself in her normal clothes, but she could now get really hurt.

"When you were little, I thought you had so much potential. I could see the many possibilities of your future. There were so many incredible pathways for you." She continued to shed the layers of armor as she spoke. "But once I saw the one, you'd take, even the amount of times I tried to re-direct you, you always chose wrong." She looked so fragile, but I knew from moments ago that fragile was something she was not.

The King stood his ground on the platform. Even with his all his Kingsmen on the ground, he looked like he would not accept defeat for an answer. "Dova my dear, I am on the throne, I did not choose wrong. I choose power," King Jett said firmly as he took a step closer. He put his hand in his pocket. I was confused as to what he was doing. I looked over at Dova as she was fully in her regular clothes now, looking much more like herself.

"Do you think you'll try and kill me now, make space for someone you deem worthy to rule?" King Jett said in a mocking tone. He smirked. I could feel that something was off. He shouldn't be happy when there would be no way he could win now.

When he pulled out his hand from his pocket, he had the same type of bracelet that was on me, Gregorio, Bondi, and Helena before. Gregorio, Bondi and I still had ours on. I immediately started to panic and tried to desperately take mine off. My wrists were small, but the bracelet was so tight. I looked at the others and no one seemed to notice his bracelet.

"No, my dear child, I don't have to kill you, the crown will do that for me," Dova said firmly.

In an instant the hooded figure next to the King stepped closer. I could feel a chill in the air. The hooded figure stood next to the King, covering their face to hide who they were and started to speak. "You seem to have missed something Dova, I have been spying on you for quite a while. And I know there is a way to reverse the Crown's doing. I am working towards mending it to be forged with power. Forged with power of the Potens." Dova gasped. There was only one person she had ever known that could infuse metals with the power to take away gifts from Potens. "Alco," she whispered. The hooded figure took his hood off to reveal himself. Alco's curly brown hair came out of the hood. He looked older now, maybe it was just exhaustion.

"Dova, Dova, Dova." He looked at the rest of them. "Gregorio, Bondi, Helena, it is good to see you all again." All of our jaws were dropped seeing this traitor as the one who had been helping the King. "You could not have seriously thought I wanted to hide in the Forest all of those years. My gift is of such importance to change this world to the way I've wanted it. Jett made me an offer I couldn't refuse. I am now his most trusted advisor," Alco said as everyone looked at him in disbelief.

He stood on the stage, looking down at all of us like we were nothing to him anymore. Helena started to put her hands together and close her eyes, to channel just enough of her gift to knock him out. She looked like she was trying so hard, but nothing was happening. She collapsed from exhaustion. Taking out all of the Kingsmen wore her out. "Helena!" I shouted as I ran towards her. "Stop trying, it's of no use," Alco said sternly. He opened his coat up to reveal a necklace underneath, that looked much like the bracelets we are all wearing.

Dova looked shocked and confused "How, how did I not see this?" Alco smirked and walked closer. "I realized that you had a blind spot in your sight – you could only see decisions that affected your life, and so until I set the Crawlers to attack the Mantel, I had not made one decision with you in mind." I tried to piece it all together- Dova had *sight*. She could witness potential fragments of the future. The idea made my head spin and yet Alco had found a way around it.

"I knew that I needed to work without you finding out. You see, a while back I discovered that I could create a metal that *takes*, and I hid the fact that I was going to use this to persuade the King to work with me. I now have that small amount of power that Helena just tried to use. Care for a demonstration?" he said with a smirk.

Alco put his hands together and focused his energy on Gregorio. Gregorio started to shake and he fell to the ground. We were all shocked witnessing this type of power. I was able to get Helena back to her feet, while she was weakened, she was still strong enough to stand.

Bondi reached over to help Gregorio while Dova stepped in front of me, putting herself as a barrier between Alco and Helena and me. "I will admit, that was a very smart move on your part. But you don't know what is about to happen now that you've made this decision. And I do," Dova said sharply. She was angry.

Out of frustration, Jett stuck his hand out and was somehow now channeling Bondi's electricity through his bracelet. Jett was human and was using the metal as a way to use Potens gift.

Bondi was shaking as the electric waves poured out of him. Gregorio had gotten back to his feet. While Alco was able to channel Helena's gift, it wasn't nearly as powerful as her own.

Bondi shook to the ground, it looked like it was draining him of his life. I screamed for Jett to stop hurting him, but it was no use. Lightning was appearing all around us, shocking all of us every step we took. Jett continued to step back as he used as much of Bondi's gifts as he could steal. Bondi was convulsing.

While the lighting surrounded us, Mikka reached on stage and grabbed Fern, helping her down to us. Jett and Alco were so focused on Bondi and the success of their creation that they weren't guarding her. We were all surrounded by Bondi's light storm that was stolen from him.

The lightning flashed, and we all knew that with one swift hit, we'd all be dead. I grabbed ahold of Mikka's hand as he held Fern close. We pulled Gregorio close to us as he started to realize the harsh reality of what was happening here. Bondi was dying right in front of us all. Gregorio was trying to use his gift but was too weak.

Watching Bondi's body drain of his gift made me sick to my stomach. We couldn't grab him because he would electrocute us, so we just stood, watching him slowly surround us with lightning until we had little space to move. Helena was trying and trying to summon her gift to show. She began to close her eyes once more.

Dova stood still, looking right at Alco and King Jett and she shouted through the rumbling thunder. "The problem with what you are doing is that no matter how hard you try, you will continue to fail."

At that exact moment, Helena had just gained enough energy back to dissolve Bondi's, Gregorio's, and my bracelet using every ounce of her gift left, which severed the connection between King Jett and Bondi. The lightning slowed to nothing until the weather around us was back to normal. Bondi collapsed to the ground. Gregorio had just enough strength to run to Bondi and pick him up.

Dova grabbed her bow and shot it at Alco's arm, knocking him over. He might have been shielded from gifts, but he was not shielded from human weapons. Alco ran into the shadows of the side of the stage like the coward he was. Dova grabbed my arm. "We have to go, now," she said calmly.

The chained Potens all began to scatter and run in all different directions. King Jett screamed loudly as he realized he had no hold over any of us anymore. Dova shot one more arrow at the King, hitting him in the leg to wound him enough to not be able to follow us. He fell to the ground. I needed my axe. I ran towards the stage to grab my axe and the dagger that he had held on the side of his suit.

He looked directly at me and looked me in the eyes as I stole my things back. "You. Evergreen. Will. Always regret this. There will not be far enough away for you to go to outrun me. I will find you and punish you for what your family did." He tried to move my hand away from taking the golden items, but he was in too much pain, bleeding out on the ground. He needed help desperately, but I did not feel sorry for him. I couldn't look back at him as I ran to join my friends, I knew the trouble we were in and we did not have much time to act.

We all ran towards what looked like a really old building. Gregorio had to carry Bondi's very weak body in order to move. The building had a ton of stairs leading up to the main entrance, but Dova led us around back to the kitchen entrance. This building must have been the Capitol building based on its size and location, but we did not have time for questions now. I would save them for later.

We went through the door and the kitchen was enormous. It had several different counters of preparation space with marble sparkling countertops. We didn't have time to marvel over the beauty as we ran quickly through the kitchen and into the dining room. We couldn't go any faster because Gregorio was carrying Bondi, Helena was extremely weak, and Fern was so little, but we were doing our best. "The guards will wake up soon, hurry!" Helena shouted as we ran through the dining room and to a door that led to a basement. We all hurried down the stairs. The basement was dark and cold and there were barrels and barrels of wine that lined the walls. This must have been the King's wine cellar for the parties and balls they used to host at the castle.

Dova led us to the very back of the basement to a wooden door that was covering a passageway. She opened the door to a dark tunnel and ushered us all through the entrance. If the basement felt cold and dark, this was worse. The chill made the hair stand up on my arms. The dark that enveloped us was the kind of dark that made having your eyes open feel like they were completely shut.

Once we shut the door behind us, we all held onto one another as we pushed ahead into the tunnel. The ground was wet and soaked our feet as we moved forward, making the cold almost unbearable, but we had to keep moving. The water splashed as we tried to run as fast as possible. I felt my stomach shake in hunger, we all hadn't eaten in over a day and we were starving. I tried to ignore my stomach as we moved forward. We did not have time for complaints, it was either move forward, or die. "Not much farther," Dova would shout every twenty or so minutes, trying to keep our spirits up I was sure.

We ran for miles and miles in this darkness. A light appeared in the distance. The light got brighter and brighter as we continued to run through the endless tunnel of darkness. As we all approached the end of the tunnel, there was yet another door. This door was made of stone with patches of grass stuffed in the cracks where the light was getting through. Dova pushed the door open without any caution whatsoever, not concerned that there would be anyone on the other side. We all followed suit as she hurried us forward. The entrance of the tunnel from the outside would have been completely hidden, it blended in perfectly with the rocks. We were surrounded by trees that were filled with a beautiful understory making it hard to see through. These trees were bigger than any I had ever seen. The trunks of the trees were larger than my wingspan.

We continued onward, through the thick of the forest until Dova stopped right in her tracks. She closed her eyes for a moment and then changed direction, heading us West of where we were now. "Not much longer," she called as we hurried in her path. After about a mile west, Dova stopped again. "Here." She pointed at a ridiculously large tree. She walked over to the tree and knocked three times. A rope ladder came falling down. She hurried us all up the ladder and she went last. Mikka and Fern were climbing up first, I was right behind them. Behind me was Gregorio pulling Bondi up the ladder while Helena tried to help and then Dova came up last.

The view from the top was an old treehouse with a green door. It was massive. The trees below completely camouflaged the treehouse from the rest of the forest. We would be safe here for now. We all moved inside as Dova knocked three times on the trunk again and the ladder rolled back up the tree, hiding our location from below. The inside of the treehouse really looked like a small home. It was all one big circular room. There was a tiny kitchen with just enough space to cook a small meal, one single armchair, made with a gift of some sort because it was crafted out of leaves and twigs, and a one-person cot that was floating off of the floor – again, gifted in some way by a Potens.

Dova closed the door behind us and she walked over to the tiny kitchen to boil some hot water so I could make a healing tea for Bondi. "Dova, what is this place?" I said quietly as I tried to help Gregorio put Bondi down to rest on the cot. I pulled out the dagger and axe that I was carrying and placed them on a small stool that was next to the cot. Gregorio was so visibly uncomfortable at the sight of his brother being in so much pain that he looked sick as well. "This is the Oak room, I had this place made a while back in case anything I couldn't see happened as a way to escape the Castle. I'm glad I did." My heart started beating faster. "What do you mean what you couldn't see?"

Dova started the fire-lit stove and waited for the water to boil. Mikka and Fern sat in the chair together, you could see how much he loved her. "I am gifted with sight, I can see the many potential futures which means I can work to manipulate them, but there was something I knew was missing. It was like every time I saw the glimmer of the future, I could tell something was not right and I could not seem to figure out what. Now I know, it was all Alco." I couldn't fathom the betrayal.

"I thought you guys saw Alco dead?" I said to Gregorio. He nodded. "He was lifeless on the floor. It was probably all an act. All part of his stupid plan," he said.

He was interrupted by the boiling water. Dova gestured towards me. "My dear Evergreen, could you make a healing tea for everyone, especially Bondi and Mikka, my cabinet should have everything you need in it." I walked over to the cabinet, confused about my grandmothers' sight, but I understood that she saw something in this particular path that made whatever outcome here seem like the best one, so I went to make the tea. I opened the cabinet door to find spices, leaves, and dried berries of all kinds. I grabbed dried monkfruit, cardamom, and a hint of jasmine leaves and willed them into the teacup. I then poured the hot water over and placed my hands around the mug to seal in my gift. I walked the tea over to Gregorio so he could get Bondi to drink it. He sat Bondi up and had him take a few sips and you could start to see his skin turn back to a normal tone. Color was coming to his skin and his cheeks. He was starting to breathe normal again. It felt like everyone in the room let out a long exhale as Bondi started to slowly gain consciousness again.

I walked over to Mikka and Fern. "Hi Fern, I've heard so much about you from Mikka, you must be so special since your brother loves you so much." She looked at me and smiled but did not say another word. She was in shock from what happened. Mikka moved her off his lap as he got up and he put her gently back in the chair. "Fern I'm going to chat with Evergreen for a moment. I'll just be over on that side of the room, you'll be able to see me perfectly fine ok?" He was trying to reassure her that he was not going to leave her. Fern nodded and we both walked over to the other side of the circular home. "My mom is dead. She died in the cells. Fern was with her and saw it all happen." He went silent as he tried to hold back his emotion. "Mikka, I am so incredibly sorry." I went to give him a hug, but he pushed me away. "Not now, I do not want her to see me upset in any way," he said firmly as he choked on those last few words trying to keep his emotions hidden.

"Understood, I'm here if you need anything," I said, not wanting to make this any harder on the two of them. Mikka nodded and leaned in to whisper something. "I don't know why the King needed her. This I need to figure out. Can you see if Dova knows anything and let me know?" I nodded.

Helena and Gregorio were watching Bondi as he began to heal. I passed tea out to everyone. We could all use it right now. Dova passed out rolls of very stale bread but we were too hungry to care. I ate my bread and walked over to Dova to ask her something that had been bothering me since earlier.

"What did you mean when you said the Crown will do it for you when you were talking to King Jett?" Dova took a sip of her tea. "Darling I don't want to involve you anymore than you already have been because it could put you in danger." She took another sip of tea. "I think it may be too late to keep secrets at this point, after all I did not even know we were family." I took a sip of my tea and the warmth started to bring me back to life as well.

"Your grandfather loved you, and the family so much. Your parents kept that secret from you because with my gift they knew you would be in danger." She took a few more sips of her tea as she paused her story. "I saw what could happen in the future, and each time I tried to change it from the old king getting killed it happened in every scenario, so your grandfather and I had a plan. With my gift, he infused the gift of sight, but the wrong type of sight, into both the Crown and the Forest of Embers. This meant that anyone who took the gold that was not rightfully theirs would find themselves always choosing the wrong path – one that would lose them money, family, friendships, and power. It is why people who steal from the forest tend to lose their things and their memory. We thought it would prevent the chaos that you see now, of the Potens being hunted down like elk." My jaw dropped as I realized that this was what the King meant earlier. They managed to change the fate of the people who stole the gold.

"The only way to change the King's fate now would for him to make amends for stealing the Crown and killing the last king or for a seer to change the fate of the gold to be the right path instead of the wrong one." I was shocked, but Dova would be the King's way of getting what he wanted. "He has been making huge changes, and trying too hard to succeed, but his path to success is twice as hard and takes twice as long. He is still in power and seeming to get what most of what he wants, but there must be something he is having trouble getting, something he wants more than anything else – I just don't know what it is." I continued to drink my tea and thought about how my grandparents were the only reason the King was not getting what he wanted. Only a few weeks ago I was sitting in my tea shop, happy and content with how my life was. But I was alone. I looked around at this room of people, friends.

"Do you know why he wants Fern?" I asked for Mikka. Dova took another sip of her tea "I believe that Fern might actually have more power than you think." I looked over at Fern, the small human. "She is human though," I said, half questioning and half sure of my answer.

"Don't be so sure. She is not fully human, nor Potens. She is something else." What did Dova mean by this. "What does that mean she is?" Dova looked down at her tea.

"She is an immortal. Mikka's parents actually lost her when she was a toddler. She was human – but she was alone in the woods for weeks. They had searched, and searched and when they finally found her, a Tree Witch had her." I gasped. Tree Witches were not something I had thought existed for centuries. They were monsters, dark and dangerous. "What did they do?" I wanted to know more. "His parents made a bargain with them – I do not know what it was, but it somehow made Fern an Immortal. I think Jett wants her to find out how to become Immortal himself. I don't think she even knows what she is."

This was all too much to process. How did Mikka not know? I couldn't talk to him here without Fern being so close to him.

I walked over to Bondi, Helena and Gregorio to check on how Bondi was doing. Bondi looked better, but was still not like himself fully. "How are you feeling?" I said in a soft voice as I wanted to see if he needed more tea. Bondi looked up at me with pain in his eyes. "I don't feel my gift anymore." His eyes started to tear up. I looked at Gregorio and then back at Bondi. "It might be because you are still feeling tired and weaker than usual, I'll get you some more tea and you can rest up." I pulled Gregorio aside as we walked toward the kitchen.

"The healing tea is supposed to be effective immediately, I think we need to consider the possibility that he is not going to use his gift at full capacity again," I whispered to him to prevent any of the others from hearing. I felt like Gregorio should know. "I can feel that something is off with him, he does not seem whole," he said. He bowed his head down to stop himself from crying in front of me. I gave him a long hug. We were both grateful that he was alive, but to be a Potens without your gift meant being stripped of a part of your identity.

Mikka was quietly talking to Fern, probably about anything other than this. Fern was only seven years old. She was so young to have gone through what she has already.

Dova handed out blankets and pillows that she had stored in the tiny closet. I took three of each and brought them over to Fern and Mikka. Everyone set up on the floor except Bondi who we all wanted to have the more comfortable cot. Outside the window, we could see the Night sky, peaking through the forest canopy. The stars twinkled in the far distance and the moon was full once again and lit up the darkness. We needed time to rest – time to reset and get ready for what was to come. We were nowhere near out of this mess yet. We blew out the candles that Dova had lit and everyone closed their eyes to sleep. I put my axe under my pillow, although I felt safe here, it made me feel home. I laid next to Mikka and looked at him as he slept in the moonlight. I was very grateful for his friendship. My eyes started too tire, and I put my head on the pillow and fell right asleep.

23

I awoke in a tent by the cliff. Here again, in this dream I couldn't seem to outrun. I grabbed my axe and walked outside by the cliff-side. I could now see the surroundings even more clearly. I looked over the edge at the waterfall and saw the river flowing fast in a direction that led through the forest beneath me into the ocean. I heard a scream, loudly but it felt closer this time. The part I knew was coming was here – I waited for the ground to crumble, but it didn't. I just wanted this part to end so my nightmare would be over, and I could wake up, but nothing came. Confused, I walked closer to the edge with my axe. I felt like I knew what I needed to do. I had an overwhelming feeling that I needed to jump. I put my axe in my backpack and jumped over the rushing waterfall and into the river. I opened my eyes.

I was back in the Oak room. I gasped for air as I awoke. "Ah, path-dreams, very interesting," Dova said as she stirred what smelled like fresh coffee on the stovetop. "What do you mean?" Dova smirked as she continued to stir the coffee around. She started to pour the coffee out into mugs for everyone. "Your grandfather and I infused the gold with that sight as I told you yesterday, but what you just showed me was that it could be tapped into if you have the gold as well. That is very interesting indeed." Dova paused for a moment and then she spoke. "What did you see?" she said.

I told her of this reccurring dream I've been having for years. I shared with her the change this time and how it felt different now. She listened and nodded. I shared how my dreams changed, ever-so-slightly and wondered what that had meant. I did not know what to make of it. Dova looked up with an intrigued look on her face. "My dear, path-dreams change as you get closer to the real event. They shift to show you more of what will actually happen. If I were you, I'd pay close attention."

I wanted to know more but we did not have enough time right now. I nodded, I got up and grabbed my cup of coffee and we all sat together and drank it.

After a night's rest and some food, we all had felt much better. Helena was sitting on the one large chair and took a moment from sipping her coffee to interrupt the silence of the morning. "We cannot run forever, and they are not going to stop looking for us. Why don't you let me kill them all?" Helena said in a monotone voice, she was not kidding. The silence that followed was so tense you could cut it with a knife.

"Because we would be no better than them." Mikka interrupted and Helena shrugged. He was right. Killing them all would make us just as bad as they were, or as they were intending to be. Fern looked terrified.

Dova intervened. "We need to find out what the King is looking for or wanting so badly, whatever it is, if we get that he won't be able to remain in power. The Crown will have him make the wrong decisions to prevent him from achieving what he desires most. If we can understand his objective, we can figure out how to stop what he is trying to do." We all looked at each other. Quietly, from behind Mikka stepped Fern. "Um excuse me?" she said in a tiny voice. "I think I might know where he was trying to go." Mikka knelt down to be closer to Fern as he spoke.

"Fern what do you mean?" She sniffled and looked like she was mustering up enough courage to tell us what she meant. "After...after mom died," she said. Her voice trailed off for a moment, she was so little to have dealt with this much death. Even though I was young when I lost my whole family, Fern felt so much more fragile than I was. "After mom died, they moved me from my cell to the Castle itself. I was given a small bedroom that was locked, but the vents in the floor were my only entertainment. I could hear everyone's conversation in the Great Room of the Castle." My jaw dropped and as I looked around the room it seemed like everyone else had thought the same. While the King was cruel, he didn't want a little girl in a cell all alone. I knew now that it was to try and find out more about how she became immortal.

Mikka looked at Fern with curious eyes. "What did you hear?" he said quietly as he wanted to make sure she felt comfortable enough to participate in this adult conversation that she was now a central part of. "Well, I heard a lot of different conversations, some about how their efforts to find something were not succeeding, some about how many towns they were trying to destroy, some about you Dova." She pointed at Dova. "They wanted Dova to fix something, they knew she would know how. They were looking to go to the Isle of Perdita. They kept saying they would find something that would help his success there. I never could quite make out enough to hear exactly what they were looking for but Jett and Frieon were always going on about transportation to that Isle." Dova started to pace slowly back and forth.

"Interesting. Well, it looks like we know where we need to go now. I have an old friend that lives by the coast that could possibly get us a boat, but it always comes with a price. I think it is worth the risk," Dova said. "I'm in, when would we leave?" Helena replied.

Dova stood by the small window next to the kitchen. As she looked outside, she spoke. "We would need to leave within the hour to get there before sunset," Dova said. Gregorio and Bondi nodded. Bondi was weak, but he would not be separated from his brother again, so whether he had his gift or not he would come with us. Plus, Mikka would be with us and he was human. I turned to look at him. He was *handsome*. What I thought was even better though was that he risked everything for his family. I was so grateful for his friendship. Mikka was looking at Fern. "I have to go with them, but I can have you stay here. This place is safe, and they won't come looking for you when they know we've all left to go somewhere else."

Fern's quiet and docile expression changed to angry. "You are not leaving me behind again, look what happened last time. I am coming with you." She demanded. Mikka looked troubled, but he knew she was right. "Ok, but on one condition. When we travel, you must do completely as I say. If I tell you to run, you run, got it?" She nodded and they shook hands. Mikka was such a good brother to her.

I started to pack a bag with the backpack Dova let me use. I put my axe in it along with some of the healing herbs and spices that were in Dova's cabinet. I took any snacks that were in the cabinet. The snacks were mostly nuts and seeds with a few slices of dried mango. I went to put the dagger that I had out on my belt and the sunlight coming through the window hit the gold that showed the inscription. "*My Dove.*" I looked over at Dova who was packing a few additional things before we headed out. "This was for you from Grandfather wasn't it?" Dova didn't say anything but she smirked, confirming what I asked.

We all got all of our bags packed and were ready to go. We went over the plan countless times before we headed out. We were to head towards the coast that was about six hours walk from here. The coastal town we were headed to was Straunton. Once there, we would see Dova's old friend, Jarano, who she said went by Jay. Jay apparently owned a boat ramp and was more of a shady person, but Dova grew up with him and knew he would help for the right price – plus, he was our only shot. After we got a boat from Jay, we would sail to the Isle of Perdita where we would spend time searching for whatever the King was looking for. After two days, whether we found it or not, we would have to return and head back to the Oak room. It would be too dangerous to search longer than that on the Isle, after all it was a small island and we would not be able to get away if we were found there when the King arrived. We all got ready to head down the rope ladder. I knocked three times on the tree and the ladder fell to the ground, ready for us to make our descent. We all headed down, nervous but ready to fight for what is ours.

24

We walked in silence for a few hours in the forest, covered by the canopy of the trees that every once in a while would let a little light peak through, warming our skin. I had my axe in my hand, ready for whatever might come our way while Gregorio had his bow ready. Mikka also had a bow – Bondi's. Bondi was too weak to really defend us right now. It was hard to watch him try and keep our pace. His sprit was hurting the most it seemed, he had tried to use his gift a few times, but nothing more than a spark happened when he could usually bring powerful lightning.

I walked over to be next to Dova, my grandmother. It still felt weird to think that she was related to me. "Dova, is it possible for Potens to have gifts they never knew of?" Dova looked at me with a confused expression on her face. "What makes you say that?" She asked as we walked along, trying to keep pace to make it to Straunton before nightfall.

"When I met Mikka and we were making the trip through the forest near my house I somehow..." I stopped because it sounded so ridiculous. How would anyone believe I floated? This was old-potens gifts, not one has been around for centuries. I had to get the answer though, Dova would know I am sure of it. "I somehow *floated.*" Dova's face did not show any surprise or shock whatsoever. She seemed like she already knew the answer.

"Ever, even though you did not know I existed, I always kept tabs on you. When I got word that you were being persecuted for killing someone, I left the Zirkel's to make sure you found some safety. I just watched you for a while, from the shadows of the forest. But when I saw you meet Mikka and could see what the future could be with him leading you to safety, I knew you were in good hands. I may have knocked down a tree, and saved you from falling, but after that I knew you'd be safe for now so I headed back to get everything set up for when you would arrive." It was Dova that knocked down that tree, it was Dova who floated me to the top. Dova must have multiple gifts that she could use at full capacity which would mean she was an untouchable. "How...are you...an untouchable?" The words came out in a loud whisper. Mikka was right behind me, hearing the whole conversation. "What is an untouchable?" he asked, wanting to learn more. Most humans were not taught about them because it could create fear of the Potens gifts. Dova answered Mikka, "Potens can use several gifts, but not at full capacity. Untouchable is a word for Potens that possess multiple gifts at once and can use them at full capacity all the time."

She took a deep breath and continued. "Since using just one gift can sometimes exhaust a Potens, using multiple energy gifts seemed like it was not possible, but there are some that don't tire. They gain energy from using their gifts which means – to certain humans – that they should not be able to live out of fear that they will try and use their gifts for power."

Mikka did not look that concerned, but it was probably because he didn't know the danger Dova would have been in if anyone knew. "How come no one found out?" We all continued walking at a brisk pace, Gregorio and Bondi at the back, Helena in front of them – holding Fern's hand and Mikka, Dova and I at the front.

Dova continued to talk, "when I was young, I knew I could use multiple gifts, but I hid the other ones from everyone. I'd pretend like I could use the other ones just a little bit, like everyone else. I realized using my sight at its full capacity would be the best gift to get me close to the King – which would keep me safe. No one will question a sightseer if they can help you conquer the things you wanted. Jett does not know. Your grandfather was the only one that knew."

I always felt jealous growing up of all the kids in my class that were able to use a gift that was much better than mine. I cannot imagine what it must have been like for Dova to possess this much power, this much talent in several gifts. I wished she did not tell us; I felt exposed knowing this secret. If anyone knew, she would be killed, or worse – used by Alco.

After we finished our conversation, the silence grew as we walked. I let Dova lead us in the direction we needed to go, and I walked alongside Mikka. My hand brushed his as we walked closely alongside one another. He looked over at me and winked. I wondered if circumstances had been different, and we weren't running for our lives, could we have been something more than just friends. But there was no time for that now. We had to focus. After another few hours of walking, we came to a road where on the other side we could see the ocean. The coast.

The sound of the waves washing up on shore interrupted our silence and the usual sounds of the forest that surrounded us. We had finally made it to the coast. I let out a breath. Step one of our plan had been completed. "Where does Jay live?" Mikka asked Dova. She looked both ways across the dirt-road and nodded for us to all cross. "He lives a mile from here – we can follow the coast the rest of the way," Dova responded once we were on the sand and hidden by bushes that lined the road.

The sun was starting to set. We had been walking for hours upon hours today. The waves crashing made it hard to hear if anyone else was there, waiting to ambush us. In the forest you could hear crunching of leaves, which would indicate if someone was truly following us or if they were getting close but here – here you could only hear the ocean's lullaby of waves. We were all exhausted and in need of some food. Mikka had put Fern on his back, this was a long walk for all of us but for her this was longer than she has ever walked at once. She was still so small.

Dova paused and we all stopped in our tracks. Up ahead was a small wooden shack that looked like it was built into the side of the shore – just far away enough from the waves to not be impacted by them, but I was sure whoever was inside would feel the spray of the ocean. Dova looked at Gregorio to gesture that she wanted his help. He nodded and used his gift to turn into a mere breeze, going ahead of all of us to look into the shack and see if we were in any danger. After just a few moments he re-appeared, in his regular form.

"Coast is clear. There is a boat ramp on the other side and a man in the shack with a hat and a long white beard. The man was sitting in a very strange rocking chair and he did not have shoes on. Was that him?" Dova smiled. "Yes, that's Jay. C'mon everyone, it's time to get our boat." Dova started to walk ahead. It was interesting to watch Dova. Dova had wrinkles on her face but a very kind smile. The tattoos on her head made me curious if there was a story behind that, but I'd have to ask another time.

We all walked with a hopeful, but anxious aura around us, knowing that whatever came ahead of this could change the fate of our world as we know it in one way or another. We approached the wooden shack. Dova lead since she knew him. When we turned the corner to see the inside of the house, we could see he was just as Gregorio described. He actually looked like a real mess. The tiny home was a disaster. It was hard to imagine how someone even made this much of a mess in this small space.

Dova knocked on the very poor excuse for a wall as she said, "hey there old friend." Jay continued rocking but slowly started to look up from the ground. His eyes were green, and they shone brightly under his wrinkly, bearded face. As he looked up his expression remained the same, steady and firm.

"My oh my, Dova. I am very surprised you would show up here after all of these years. I had always wondered if I would ever see you again. It's been years too long." Dova smiled and walked over as Jay stood up and she gave him a big hug.

Jay sat back down right away as he said, "who are your friends?" It seemed like he knew there would be a big reason why Dova would be here. He was curiously looking around at all of us. He reached beside his small table that was an old wooden box that looked like it probably washed ashore from a large ship and grabbed a warm can of what looked like beer and cracked it open.

Dova looked at him and said, "they are my family – in one way." She did not share any other crucial information, instead she just stopped at that. But he seemed skeptical, knowing that there would be much more to what she said. "Well, if they're your *family*, welcome. Help yourself to a beer, or whatever you'd like." We all shook our heads no, but we all sat down while Gregorio stayed leaned against the shack as a lookout on the outside. It was a long journey to get here, and we knew we had so much farther to go – but it felt nice to rest for a moment.

"I know you wouldn't be here if you didn't need something, so out with it," Jay said with a curious tone. It seemed like he was trying to pry into what she was doing here. I didn't like the way he was looking at Dova, I wanted to say something but we really needed his help so there was no point in making things awkward. "You *my friend* are right. We are in need of a boat for two days' time. We will bring the boat back and we are willing to pay. The only thing is I cannot tell you what we need it for and cannot provide any details about it when we get back, only that it will be returned to you in perfect condition," Dova said this with confidence but then her face changed, and she felt conflicted. I wondered if she could see what his answer would be. "Well, well, well. Although I'd love to help, I don't think any of you would have enough to actually pay me for a private boat rental, especially when I am confident that there is something illegal going on here. Especially when I got news earlier today that you were wanted and to report immediately if you were found." He looked up at Dova.

He sipped another large swig of his drink and sat further back in his chair. I looked at Dova who looked very unbothered, like she already knew he was not going to report her. Jay kept rocking in his chair. "What are you willing to give up?" he said in a very calm tone.

I could feel the air shift around us, it went from feeling warm and inviting to feeling cold and unnerving. I couldn't tell what was making it that way, or if I was the only one noticing it, but when I looked at Fern, she was trying to make herself warm, so I knew it was not just me. Dova answered. "I can see what your price will be, and it is a no." I looked at Mikka confused, but Dova must have known something we did not. "Well, that's that then. It was nice seeing you Dova," Jay said as he continued to rock and drink his beer.

"Wait. What is the price, I might be willing to pay it?" Mikka stood up and asked for more information. Dova put her hand on her shoulder and shook her head no. She seemed to not want anyone to know what it would be. Jay put his feet down to stop rocking in his chair. He took another sip of his drink and he looked up right at Mikka and said, "I'm going to need a trade and a promise." Mikka looked at Dova, not sure why that was a bad offer. "What did you want to trade and what kind of promise?" Mikka said, wanting to learn more.

Jay took another sip of his drink and looked quickly at Dova and then at me. "I want that girls axe as my trade, and I want a blood oath." Bondi let out a gasp behind me. Mikka, Fern and I seemed to be the only ones in the room that had no clue what that meant. "The blood oath I want is that if my boat did not come back the way it was promised, I could have one of you in my debt for life. You could pick who, but that promise would mean that I would *own* your blood for life." Mikka looked defeated, he knew we wouldn't be able to take that sort of risk. I also did not want to give up my golden axe. Dova turned to look at the ocean. She was staring into the distance when I walked up to her.

The rest of the room was quietly whispering about what options we'd have now. We had traveled so far to get here and did not have that much time until we would need to move again. Without a boat, we would not be able to get to the Isle of Perdita. "Dova, what now?" I whispered to her as she stared into the sunset and the blanket of stars started to appear above us, one by one they twinkled to signal nighttime. A tear streamed down her face and she wiped it away. "Is everything ok?" Dova nodded. "Yes, my dear, I have a plan." Dova turned around and walked right back at Jay. "We will trade you her golden dagger instead of the axe and I will take the blood oath." We all gasped, and mouths were jaw-dropped all over the room.

Gregorio interrupted. "Dova no. We will find another way, it is not worth it." Dova looked at Gregorio and seemed to have communicated something with him that she did not say out loud. He nodded and looked down with a sad expression on his face. "Shake on it." She demanded Jay. I grabbed the dagger out of my belt and Jay's face lit up in surprise – pure gold. He went to reach for Dova's hand, but she pulled back for a moment. "Promise me this, if something is to happen to me, the blood oath is done. It ends with me. That is the only way I will take this deal." He shrugged and reached his hand back out. "Deal." Once they shake, the fate is sealed. We must bring this boat back in the condition we got it in and in just two days' time.

Jay walked us all over to his boat ramp and there is an old-but beautiful large sailboat that would be perfect for us. It had bigger sails than any I had ever seen in person, after all Kinver wasn't on the water. We all got in, one by one as Mikka picked Fern up to get her in the boat. Gregorio untied the lines from the dock and released the sails and we all sailed out into the blanket of twinkling darkness.

25

It had been a few hours of rocking on the sea. I had never been on a boat before and I felt horrible. Every few minutes I would get up and throw up off the side of the boat. I felt like I would rather be stuck back in that prison than on this endless rocking nightmare. Mikka came over to comfort me every once in a while, but I could not keep anything down. I did not even have anything left in my stomach. Gregorio and Bondi maneuvered the boat, adjusting the sails to head towards our intended direction. Helena sat at the very front of the boat on the bow, watching what was ahead of us. Dova sat with Fern and told her stories to occupy her from being scared of sailing on the boat.

When I finally felt like I could sit without feeling nauseous, Mikka sat down with me. I was so tired from being sick that I rested my head on Mikka's shoulder. Mikka grabbed my hand gently as we sat together under the moving starline as we all sailed into the night. We sat in complete silence, but I wished things could be different with him. Mikka made me feel like I was important, like I had family at last, but I did not know how to tell him that, so I said nothing.

There was so much more at stake than us here – there was humanity as we know it.

After a while longer, Helena pointed ahead. "The Isle of Perdita," she said in a monotone voice. Not many people got to see the Isle of Perdita and it was way bigger than I could have imagined.

It was difficult to get to, and not many people owned their own boats to sail here. Nor would anyone want to – this place was doomed. The Isle stretched so wide it was hard to take it all in from the boat. It was still dark out, but dawn would be here soon, we had to hurry if we wanted to get there before light. The Isle was uninhabited, no one lived there, it was just a jungle island filled with creatures that were not permitted back on the mainland. The fact that we had not seen some of these creatures, even in pictures, made this more frightening, but I also dreaded the fact that we would only have daylight to look for whatever it was that the King wanted to find here. This would be the most difficult, knowing that we did not even have enough information to know where to look on the Isle.

The darkness that surrounded the Isle was not just the night sky but a dark fog that encapsulated the surroundings. We sailed through it, engulfing ourselves into the fog. The Isle appeared in front of us. It felt wrong to be here, in my gut I knew this was not a great idea, but we were out of all the other options. Plus, I would literally do anything to get off this boat. The brothers slowed the boat down as we landed slowly on shore. The boat slowly jolted as it slid up against the shoreline, but it almost knocked me off my feet. The sun should rise soon, the thought of that comforted me.

We all gathered around Dova to find out what it is we would do next. I didn't think any of us really anticipated that we would get this far. "We need to find something that the King would need, something that would make him more powerful than anyone else, a power so strong it would break the Crown's curse. I've been thinking this through for the entire night and I think he is looking for an

Industria crystal. I have never seen one, but if there was any still left, they would definitely be here." I looked at Dova. "What is that and what does it do?" Dova looked over my shoulder towards the shoreline. "In olden times, there were many ways Potens became more powerful, and one of those ways was to use these crystals to enhance the gifts they already had. The old King banned them because they made certain Potens too powerful, but most of the crystals that were out there were small, pocket sized crystals. Whatever he's looking for would have to be much bigger than that. With that crystal and Alco's creation that can take gifts from other Potens, the King would be unstoppable as a human, maybe even more powerful than any Potens alive. My hope is that the Crown will not guide him here before us, it is, after all, supposed to make him miss what is most desirable to him." Mikka interrupted before Dova could say anymore. "Well, how do find it?" Dova's face changed. "I am not sure. I don't even know if that is what he was looking for, but it is all I could think of. I tried to think of anything from long-ago that would be out here –"

"I know how to find that, but you are all not going to like it." Bondi stopped Dova from continuing any further with her sentence. "These crystals, I've seen one. The energy that is within them radiates outward. They were not just banned because they were powerful, they were also banned because they attracted all sorts of creatures. They brought Crawlers out of the forest, monsters like you've never seen before would come right out of the sea. People who possessed even the smallest crystal would find themselves followed by these things. If there is one of them on the Island, we find it by finding where all the creatures lurk."

Great. The thing I wanted to avoid on this Island was running into the King's Guard or creatures of some sort and this was what we would have to do. "Well, we don't really have any choice now. We have only around 18 hours to get out of here and head back before we would be too late." Onward was the only choice. We only had two days with the boat and the travel here had taken up too much time. We all agreed that it would be best to go now before it was too late. We had a time limit on the boat and the cost of borrowing was too steep to miss that limit.

We all got off of the boat and headed into the darkness. It was still dark, no sign of the sun rising which was weird considering it was definitely after dawn. The darkness did not stop our plans, it just made us move a little faster in fear of what hid in the darkest shadows. Especially since we had to find where the creatures would be.

We gave everyone, even little Fern a weapon. She had a small knife to use in case of an emergency. We all tried carefully not to make a lot of noise. We came up with very basic hand signals to use in order to prevent anyone from needing to talk as we moved into the darkness. We headed forward, keeping our eyes out for anything that might move. As much as I didn't want to run into anything, this felt like the only way to actually find the crystal. I hoped that the crystal was what the King was looking for. We would only have one shot at this.

The forest was unlike the one on the mainland, the trees bent in very different directions and were all covered in a mossy texture. It felt much damper in here, even the ground was seeped with water which slowly rose up with each step, covering the bottoms of all of our shoes. The sound of each step we took made noise, but was masked by the sounds of the creatures lurking around us – the ones we could not see, but could feel and hear their presence.

After about thirty minutes into our walk, Bondi signaled to pivot left. I was not sure what he could see but after this he kept changing directions every few minutes, moving us swiftly from one way to another, following something that I did not know or could not see. Dova stopped immediately. It almost looked like she had run into a wall. She closed her eyes and after a few moments that stretched to what felt like a lifetime, she opened her eyes. She signaled for everyone to continue onward. It was too dangerous right now to ask out loud what she saw but we all knew if it was bad, she would not have told us to continue. Bondi continued to track whatever it was that he was following, I couldn't see what it was. Everyone stayed quiet and kept out eyes peeled for any movement in the forest. The ground started to shake from underneath us. Dova looked over and signaled something to Helena.

Fern grabbed Mikka's arm and she let out a loud enough shriek to wake the whole forest. Out from the solid, wet ground right in front of her grew a huge creature. I had never seen anything like it, the body was black but shined blue in the light of my flashlight. In all but an instant, Mikka jumped in front of her, shielding her from this wild creature. Bondi and Gregorio started to fire arrows at it while Mikka had his sword drawn, blocking it every time it tried to strike him like a snake would. Helena's eyes glowed red and she shook for a moment and the creature shook as well. It started swaying its long-blue, scaled body as it started to faint. Mikka pulled Fern out of the way before the creature's body slammed to the ground. Looking at its lifeless body, it had several legs that were hidden under the surface. The teeth were each the size of a large dagger. And its breath was unbearable. A chill went down my spine looking at it.

"What was that?" I said, breathing heavily as my heart raced at a swift pace for those few minutes. Dova walked over. "That was a creature I did not know still existed. They used to call those Terraportens. They are huge, but can live in water the size of a small puddle. One bite and the person slowly loses their mind, it makes them forget who they were and who anyone is. That is if they only take one bite, otherwise they eat people whole. They were all said to have been hunted and killed hundreds of years ago." Dova said as she brushed off her robe. "Clearly that was not the case. We have to keep moving, there could be much more dangerous creatures in here than that."

She pointed to the lifeless Terraportens. "More dangerous than that?" I whispered. Dova nodded. I walked over to Fern to see if she was ok. Fern was silently crying. I kneeled down for a moment to check on her. "You ok little one?" I said as I wiped the tears off of her cheek. She nodded. She was too afraid to speak. I looked up at Mikka as he helped me back up. The touch of his hand sent a chill down my spine. I wanted to say out loud what I was thinking, to tell him I wanted to kiss him – even if it could never happen now, I yearned to. I let the thought go, there was no time to wish for these kinds of things now.

Once I was up, we all made sure to gather our things so that nothing was left behind. Bondi was examining the creature. I was not sure what he was looking for, but he was very concentrated on the tail. After a few moments Bondi signaled for us to follow.

We all followed after him as he seemed to know where he was going. We moved through bushes, more swampy areas that were so deep we had to put Fern on Mikka's shoulders so she would not drown. We trekked through river crossings that Dova had to will some of us over with the fear that we would be swept away, or worse, there could be creatures underneath. All of this while it was still dark which was strange considering it had been hours since we first arrived. Dova walked alongside Bondi, her bald head covered in tattoos really made her look fierce even though she had wrinkles. I felt proud that she was my grandmother, it felt good to have some sort of family around.

Bondi stopped and sniffed the air really loudly, like he was trying to smell for something. He gestured for us all to be quiet, which meant quieter than ever considering none of us had been talking for hours. He motioned for us to sit down slowly so we did.

I felt my heart start racing, I could hear the sound of my heart-beat in my ears because out of nowhere the entire forest went silent. It was an eerie kind of silence. I could hear my breath now as well. I was not sure what we were waiting for, but I did not want to find out. A noise started buzzing in the distance, we all huddled to-gether, crouched down like Bondi instructed. The buzzing started to get louder and louder until it felt like it was right on top of us. Fern was squeezing her eyes shut, as tight as she could to keep from see-ing what was above us.

Mikka was holding her hand. I slowly started to shift my gaze up to see what it was. A swarm of what looked like bees were overhead, except they weren't bees. They had glistening fangs, were three times the size of bees, and they glowed making them look like twinkling stars.

Gregorio shifted in an instant into air and wind, he created a wind that started to push the buzzing monsters out from above us and back into the trees. The buzzing was loud because it seemed to have angered them, but Gregorio's gift was slowly shoving them away from us, making the buzzing noise softer and softer until it was gone. After ten minutes of silence, a wind surrounded us, blow-ing the hair in front of my face as Gregorio appeared once again. The noises around us resumed, like the forest had come back to life. Bondi whispered, "we have to almost be there." No one spoke of what those bee-like creatures were and onward we went once again.

We moved swiftly, starting to quicken our pace even though it was exhausting. Although it was pitch-dark out, way ahead we could see a purple glow, lighting the surrounding environment in lumines-cence. The trees almost sparkled near it. It was difficult to shift my gaze anywhere else. We got closer and closer until Bondi signaled us to stop and nodded toward Gregorio. Gregorio used his gift and shifted back into a mere breeze as he went to see what was ahead. I gripped my axe with one hand. Mikka was on the other side of me, holding Fern's hand. Helena was right behind all of us, guarding our back if anything came our way. Bondi and Dova were still at the front, waiting for Gregorio's return. Gregorio appeared, out of breath but in one piece. "The Industria crystal, it's there, but you are not going to be happy about it."

26

We all were eager to hear what Gregorio had seen. We got him some water and then leaned in to listen to what he had to say. "The crystal is HUGE! I mean like the size of a large boulder – which means we will have no way of getting it off this Island. The other problem is that there are Crawlers surrounding it. The energy it is emitting is warm, and with no sun in sight, this seems to be their only source of heat," he said.

Helena walked over to whisper, "How many of them?" Gregorio nodded his head and said, "too many to count, I've never seen that many in one place. They are bigger than the ones on the mainland, I think the crystal is giving them more power." How would we get this thing away from those creatures and off the Island? The boat couldn't possibly carry the weight of the crystal. I had to think of some solution. Everyone was quietly thinking of a potential plan.

I thought for a moment and then it hit me. "Gregorio is there a water source they are using?" Helena moved closer to see where I was going with this. "Yes, next to the crystal is a large pond that some of them were drinking from...why?" he asked out of curiosity.

I pulled my pack off my back and put it down on the ground. I pulled some spices and herbs out of my pack along with a small pot that I had taken from Dova's place. I started to add some of my water from my bottle to the pot and quietly began stirring my spices and herbs into it. I placed my hands around the pot and began to will my gifts into it. "Helena, could you heat the pot?" Although I was skilled at tea making, I could never will warmth from my hands like most average Potens. Helena kneeled down beside me and did what I asked. "You know, this is not an ideal time to make tea Evergreen," she said as I continued to stir the heated pot.

"You are absolutely right, but it is a good time to make a sleeping draught." I kept stirring. Dova smirked, and everyone seemed to have figured it out. Fern though, walked up and asked, "What are you going to do with this?" she said in a very timid, quiet voice. "I'm going to poison their water source. It should make them sleep for a day or two and we will have time to figure out what to do with the crystal." Everyone was in agreement. This would be the best solution. It would also buy us some time.

After the tea was made, we had to decide how to bring it over to the water source. Gregorio couldn't carry it while he was using his gift so that was out of the question. "I could go, I can drop one of them if I am caught." Helena suggested but Dova was shaking her head no. "If you leave and something happens to you, we lose our best protection for our group, we cannot risk it," Dova said with no hesitation. She was right.

We looked around for a moment, Bondi could not go, he still wasn't fully better, and his gift was nowhere to be found within him. Mikka stood up. "I'll go." He volunteered himself for the job. Fern kept pulling on his shirt whispering "No, no you promised you wouldn't leave me again." Mikka looked at her and put his hand on her shoulder. "I know, but it is only for a little while, and once I am back, we will be able to get off this Island." Fern was crying.

"No, I'll go," I interrupted. "It's my tea so I should be the one to do it." Dova smiled with pride. I may not have the greatest gifts, but I had to protect my family.

I started to tighten my shoelaces. I poured the rest of my water into Mikka's bottle and poured my tea into my bottle. One sip and those large creatures would be knocked out for days. With a human, this sleeping draught could knock you out for months. Dova reached in her robe to pull out a small woven bag that would wrap over my chest to hold the bottle in place. "How did you know I'd need this?" Dova smiled and walked away. Of course, she knew, she can see fragments of the future, so she probably packed for all the potentials.

Mikka walked over towards my spot as I was preparing for what was to come. "Thank you, for everything," he said as he kissed my forehead. My entire body felt like lightning. His touch made me feel unlike anything I had ever felt.

I felt like the entire world around us was no longer there, and all that mattered was this moment. I nodded. I couldn't possibly tell him how I felt, my voice wouldn't even come out. My nerves were through the roof. I had to get through this next step and then maybe, just maybe I could tell him how I felt. I grabbed my axe, carried the tea in my bottle in the woven bag Dova gave me and got instructions from Gregorio on the layout. I headed out towards the crystal.

Before I could get too far Helena caught up to me. "Wait," she whispered. Helena leaned down and picked up the muck on the ground and started smearing it on my arms. "What are you doing?" I asked. She started spreading it all over my body. "They won't smell you with this on, it is to prevent them from finding you." She put out her hands with the muck in them and I grabbed some to rub on my face and head. "Thank you." She nodded and went back to the group. I headed on.

The glowing light shimmered on everything around it, making the wonky looking trees sparkle and enticing. I still couldn't see the crystal, from the back the rocks and trees that protected it, keeping it concealed were all around it, covering its view from this side. I walked into what was certain to be my death if I made too much noise. I started to approach the back end of the crystal from behind, just like Gregorio told me.

Out of nowhere a Crawler was walking right toward me. I held my breath as it approached. So much larger than the ones I saw in the Zirkel's. So many teeth. I couldn't focus on anything but his teeth. The monster itself was surprisingly furry, the fur almost had a black shimmer to it. I only noticed the fur because it hung over some of the teeth. Each tooth was two feet long. I wanted to sink into the earth to get away from this thing.

I closed my eyes, in fear that the blinking would make it obvious that I was alive. I gripped my axe like I never have before, ready to strike if I was made. The creature leaned in toward me, and sniffed me, waiting to see if I was food or just part of the landscape. I needed to breathe but I couldn't, I knew my breath would give me away. The Crawler slowly turned around and began to walk away. I breathed out.

My heart was pounding, but I would have to thank Helena for the muck idea later. I continued to quietly step closer to the crystal. When I turned the corner, I saw what Gregorio meant. There was an incredible number of Crawlers. As awed as I was about the Crawlers, the crystal made it difficult to look at anything else. It was massive. It almost looked like something was swimming in it with the way it sparkled, it looked like it was *living*. The warmth that the crystal gave off made it very obvious as to why the creatures wanted to be near it.

I shook my head to focus back on the task at hand. About thirty feet in front of me was the pond, it was shimmering purple as the light from the crystal reflected off the surface. I slowly stepped, one step at a time towards it. There were too many Crawlers to make a mistake now. Even with my axe, I'd be done for if just one of them were to attack me. I slowly got close enough to pour the large mixture of sleeping tea into the pond. I unscrewed the lid of the bottle and slowly dumped it into the water to not make a sound for anyone to hear.

There were a few Crawlers already drinking the water and the sleeping draught would take effect within two minutes. I turned to count the Crawlers to get an idea of what we would be against. Thirty, thirty-five, forty-two. Forty-two massive Crawlers. I slowly moved backwards, one step at a time, glancing over my shoulder to ensure that I would not step on anything. My heart was racing, but I did it. With each step I felt like I could breathe more easily.

I finally could see my friends in sight and walked over to them and dropped to my knees. That was easily the most terrifying thing I had ever had to do. Mikka handed me his water and encouraged me to drink as much as I needed, even though we did not have a lot left. I drank some water and then stood up and walked over to Helena. I put my hand on her shoulder and quietly said, "Thank you." She looked away.

Helena didn't seem to like being recognized, she knew she had a strong gift, but preferred life in the shadows rather than the spotlight. She was not humble by any means, but she didn't like praise. "Don't mention it," Helena said back as she moved my hand off her shoulder.

"How long do we need to wait?" Bondi said as he pulled out some snacks from one of the bags to pass them around. We were all hungry. "I would think about an hour since we have to wait until they all drink the water." I started to wipe the muck off my face and onto my pants. Mikka passed me some dried fruit and I ate some as we all sat down.

We all faced different directions so in case anything else tried to approach us we would be able to warn one another. Mikka sat next to me while Fern sat next to Dova. Dova was comforting Fern, talking to her about anything other than what we were currently doing. I felt like this was my moment. I did not know if we would make it off this Island, so I wanted to tell Mikka how I felt. I looked at him, his beautiful blue eyes that shone, even in the darkness of the Island. I was about to speak when he interrupted my thought.

"Evergreen, that was really brave what you did back there, and I know you did it so Fern wouldn't worry about me, so thank you." Mikka whispered as we all continued to try and be as quiet as possible. "Not a problem," I whispered back. I did not know why I could not seem to muster up the courage to tell him how much he meant to me but every time I turned to tell him, it felt like there was a lump in my throat. After a long while of all of us sitting there in silence, Gregorio used his gift to check on the Crawlers. I turned to Mikka once more. "Mikka I..." Gregorio appeared. "It is time," he said.

We all stood up and started heading over to the crystal. We took the same route as I did before. We approached the crystal with wonder as it was so hard to take your eyes off it. All the Crawlers were fast asleep. We had plenty of time considering they would be asleep for a few days with that sleeping draught.

We all stood in front of the crystal. The sheer size of it was overwhelming to look at. It glimmered and looked so alive. "How are we going to get this off the Island. How is the King planning on getting this off the Island?" Bondi said. "I don't think anyone can get this off. I feel like we are missing something here," Gregorio said back.

Dova intervened. "I know that my vision a few hours ago showed this very crystal, I am not sure how he is planning on using it though, it doesn't seem to be decided yet." Mikka spoke up. "What if we destroyed it instead?" "It isn't a bad idea, but how is the real question," I spoke. Mikka took the golden axe out of my hand and slammed it into the crystal with enough force to completely knock him off of his feet.

It made a loud clanging noise that probably could have been heard on the mainland. "What are you doing!?" I shouted at him. "Trying to destroy it, you said they were asleep." He pointed at the sleeping Crawlers. We all looked up at the crystal and it did not even make a dent. How were we supposed to destroy this? "Dova, how did they destroy these in the past?" Dova looked puzzled, she always seemed confident in her next steps but this time it felt like she was genuinely confused. "I had heard stories of Potens that possessed power to dissolve, kind of like one of Helena's power. Helena, why don't you try to dissolve it." Helena's eyes glowed red. She put her hands together to get the right amount of strength. She concentrated hard and immediately fell backwards. The crystal remained the same. She dusted herself off and stood back up. "What if I…" She walked toward the crystal. Helena placed one hand on the crystal and closed her eyes. "HELENAA NO," Dova shouted from her gut, she saw what was about to happen, but it was too late.

Helena tried to use the power of the crystal to enhance her power to destroy it, but it lit up so brightly, it was blinding. The next thing I saw when I opened my eyes was the crystal, standing just like it was and Helena lying on the ground next to it. I ran to her to check if she was still breathing. She still had a pulse, but barely. "What do we do," I shouted through my tears. I did not want to lose her. Bondi said in a very soft voice, "Mikka pick her up, we have to go, NOW." The Crawlers around us started to wake up. The sleeping draught I made must not have been strong enough with the energy they've gained from the crystal. "RUN," Gregorio shouted.

Mikka threw Helena over his shoulder and Gregorio grabbed Fern's hand. We all started running but then a Crawler jumped right in the middle of our group, separating me and Dova from the rest of them. I signaled for them to run. "Go to the boat!" I shouted as Dova and I ran the other way. We ran through the trees as Dova was dropping tree by tree in the Crawler's path. We could no longer see the rest of our group, or the Crawler. We stopped for a moment to catch our breath. "Are you ok?" I asked Dova, knowing she must be out of breath from using her gift the entire run. "I'm fine sweet Ever."

We continued on as the terrain got steeper and steeper. We knew we were going the wrong way, but we wanted to get some distance between us and that Crawler. As we continued to hike up, the dense dark fog that encapsulated the island started to dissipate at this altitude, and we could see that the sun was out, but it was almost sunset now. We were running out of time. As we got almost to the top of the peak, we saw there was a cliff edge. A river flowed by, down the cliff edge, creating a waterfall into the ocean. The river defied all I knew about gravity, as it flowed up and over the edge of the cliff. Something about all of this felt very familiar. We walked over to the cliff edge to see if we could see the boat, but the dense fog covered all sight of the shoreline from here. I looked over at Dova, but she sat down. "Dova what are you doing? We have to go now." She nodded. "No, my dear, this is where it ends for me."

27

I was very confused. I felt like I had been here before. My stomach started to drop. "Dova if you're tired rest for a little but then we need to go." I looked at the cliff edge while she sat, axe in my hand ready to defend us if needed. Out of the woods appeared Alco. "Ah, just who I was looking to find," Alco said. Behind him appeared six Kings guards.

"How, how did you find us." I stuttered over my words as I stepped in front of Dova as she continued to sit on the ground in protest of leaving. "Did you think we would be that stupid to lose you? No, we had followed you to see if you could lead us to what we were looking for." Dova started to get up. "Yes, but you won't get it off the Island," Dova said as she got to her feet. Alco let out a low laugh. "The crystal, you thought we were looking for that. How intriguing. Dova your mistaken on so many levels. It seems, your gift is not what it used to be," he said as he stepped closer.

He reached into his coat jacket and pulled out an old book. "No, my dear, we were looking for this and it is you that won't be getting off this Island, but you already knew that didn't you." I was completely unaware of what book he was holding but Dova seemed disgusted. The book was ancient, the cover had writing on it that I could not quite make out and a drawing of a crown. Dova looked at Alco with disappointment. "How could you betray me like that Alco? After all these years that I took care of you. Even when no one else wanted to, I did. You should be truly ashamed of yourself." Alco looked angry.

"It is your fault. You didn't want to see my full potential. You did not want me to become who I am. But the King, he is smart, he sees me for what I am and what I can become." He put the book back into his coat. Dova looked at him and asked, "How were you able to find the book?" Alco looked at Dova, happy he outsmarted her. "The King started to realize that if he transferred his power to others, he could find what he was looking for. He gave me the power to channel other Potens energy which had helped me tap into yours." Dova looked stunned, she seemed as if she did not know that there was a way around what her and Siron had set up, as if she was truly outsmarted. "Oh, and if you think we won't find Fern, you're wrong. We will get what we need." Fern would forever be in danger unless we found a way to stop them. My mind raced on all the things we can try to do to escape this moment, to just get another chance.

He stepped closer. "BACK UP," I shouted at him and he let out a low laugh. Dova stepped in front of me. "Evergreen I love you. Even if you did not know me, I watched you. I saw you grow up into the kind, courageous person you are today – and I am very proud of you. If I saw a better way, we could have taken it but this is how this needs to end," she said.

It all took one minute as I had realized that this was the nightmare I had been having, I was here in real life. Alco pulled out a sword and stabbed it right through Dova as she screamed. Her voice was the one I had been hearing. Tears swelled up in my eyes. 'NOOOOOOOOOO,' I screamed as Dova fell to the ground her blood spilling out into a pile that was seeping into the river below, changing the water from blue to red.

I picked up my axe to swing it at Alco, and he blocked it with his blade. I continued to swing and swing until I was exhausted, him blocking my every move. "Give up Evergreen. You have nowhere to go." But I did - I had this dream before, I had somewhere to go. I knew what needed to happen next. "You're wrong. You will regret this." With tears in my eyes, I looked back at Dova's body, I loved her too, even if it was only for a short while. I turned toward the edge of the river that flowed into a waterfall. I sprinted towards the cliff and jumped off, axe in hand, holding it tightly as I fell down, down, down. I closed my eyes as I fell, and soared through the air, through the dense fog below and into the ocean.

The water hurt so bad when I plunged into it. It felt like I had hit cement completely knocking the wind out of me. I pulled myself together, axe still somehow in hand and started to swim away from the base of the waterfall. The axe was making it hard to swim but I would not let that go, this was the last thing I have to remember my family. *My family.* I lost the only family I had left – all in an instant. My heart had felt heavy, but I had to keep going.

I continued to swim out to sea, I could not go back to the Island this unprotected. Alco probably assumed I was dead anyways, but the creatures on the island would not. I could see the sailboat out in the distance, just far enough from the shoreline that I could probably make it. I had to keep up my strength.

Each stroke was harder than the last, but knowing my friends were on that boat made each stroke that much more important. Bondi shouted, "Port side!" As Gregorio shifted the sails to move closer to me. "Heave her up Mikka." I choked on the water I had inhaled as I swam. Mikka pulled me up over the side of the boat. Helena was awake but lying down. She must have been so drained from what happened earlier to her. But everyone was here safe. Everyone except Dova.

"Where's Dova?" Gregorio blurted out, in fear of the answer he already knew. "She didn't make it. It was Alco," I said as I started to weep. Silence filled the air as everyone realized one of the greatest Potens of all time was gone – and she was also our friend, *our family*. Little Fern started to cry.

"Alco, Alco was *here*?" Gregorio asked with anger behind his intention. "Yes, and they have what the King needed. It was not the crystal, it was a book. It must have been hidden near the crystal for protection knowing that no one would try and take it with all the creatures that reside there," I said as I cried and tried to get my heart rate back to normal. "What was the book?" Bondi asked as he steered us into the sunset. "It had ancient writing on it, and a picture of a crown. But I have no idea what it was," I said as I looked over at the water.

Bondi and Gregorio looked at each other with morbid facial expressions. Bondi spoke, "I know what the King wants to do. He is going to raise the dead." Mikka interrupted. "Wait what. What do you mean?" Gregorio's stunned face makes us all nervous. "That book, the book of Viempro was written by a Potens who was driven to acquire power. Viempro had created a way to raise dead Potens and channel their power as his own. He tried to obtain several dead opponents' gifts, but a group of powerful Potens rose up against him and killed him. The King at the time hid the book so no other Potens would be able to find it, because with it, they could bring Viempro back and use his power too."

Mikka asked with hope in mind, "Well, could this book bring people we wanted back?" I knew what he meant, his mom, Dova, anyone we had all lost along the way. Gregorio shook his head. "It doesn't actually bring them back to life, they stay dead, but they are given a lifeforce energy that allows any gifts to be stolen or used while they stay that way. Their bodies are lifeless, just the energy from their gifts that is taken. It is cruel to the dead to do this to them – and does a great disservice to their families if they have to see them like that, decaying and rotting." I paused for a moment and felt a full sense of dread come over my entire body. I knew what could happen next.

"Dova...they have Dova's body. They can bring her back and see the future." Bondi gasped and we all looked at one another. The shock of the realization that if they could use Dova's power, they could break the curse of the Crown filled the entire boat with hopelessness.

Helena sat up, weak but still enough energy to say what she wanted to. "We cannot give up this easily. They may have the book, and Dova, but we have something better. We have each other, and we cannot let this be the end of this fight." I was shocked that Helena was this spirited, it seemed to me that we had lost. "I have an idea – we sail to the Coast of Jericho. That is where I grew up. There is someone there that might be able to help us. We can still find a way to win," she said with determination. Bondi and Gregorio looked at each other and nodded. I stood up and looked at all of my friends. "We have nothing left to lose, lets head to Jericho."

28

I stood at the balcony, overlooking the vast ocean, knowing all that I had left behind. My tea shop, the comfort of the life I had been living, the only family I had left, and my cozy little house. I had left it all and it would never be the same again. I stood there for a while as I pondered everything as tears streamed down my face at the losses we all suffered. Footsteps sounded from behind me. It was Mikka.

"Hey, you doing ok?" he asked as he stood next to me. Gregorio was still steering the sailboat from the stern, but everyone else was asleep. The darkness was broken up by bits of twinkling starlight above. The moon was bright and shimmered on the reflection of the ocean. "I'm going to be ok. I'm really sorry about your mom. I feel like we haven't had any time to talk about that." He looked down for a moment, maybe I shouldn't had said anything. I felt his hand brush against mine and he intertwined his fingers in mine. I felt completely defeated from the day, but in holding his hand I felt like everything was going to be ok.

"Evergreen I truthfully did not expect to ever see either of them again, but you made that possible. These past few weeks with you despite all of the hurt and pain we've had to endure you've been by my side. You've trusted me, helped me, and even when you had every opportunity to leave you stayed anyway to help me find my family." Mikka turned toward me and grabbed my hips to turn me to face him as well. My heart raced as he looked at my eyes. He brushed his hand on my cheek and slowly pulled my face closer to his. I could feel his breath on my skin. He leaned in and placed his lips on mine. Home. I had felt home.

We both held hands and turned to look back at the ocean. "We are going to get through this, together," I said. And so, we sailed off into the night, hopeful for a new dawn to rise, and for us to rise with it.

ACKNOWLEDGMENTS

Thank you to my family, especially my Dad, Hal, who spent hours on the phone with me talking over the story. Without his encouragement, I could not have completed this book when I did. I will always cherish and appreciate the time he spent editing the book and giving suggestions on additions to make the story what it is today.

A huge thank you to my Husband Mike who listened to me on countless road trips talking about the plot, the characters, and how excited I was to bring the idea to life. He let me bounce ideas off of him and gave me constant support on writing this story.

TURN THE PAGE FOR A PREVIEW OF THE NEXT
BOOK IN THE SERIES.

COMING JAN. 2023

The day was dreary. The waves continually rocked the boat. I thought I had hated sailing before, but this, this was unmanageable. "Are we almost there?" I shouted through the howling of the wind. The rain had picked up again, drenching us all from all sides.

"Almost!" shouted Helena. We had been on the boat for six days now, I wanted to jump off. I sat with my back leaned against the side of the boat as I held my head into my knees and cried. The weight of it all was coming down on me. We lost Dova, my tea shop, my life, and now we had to find some sort of miracle in order to somehow beat the King.

I felt defeated. Dealing with anxiety my whole life meant constantly overthinking about little things, but this was actual danger.

Gregorio and Bondi tried to direct the sails, trying to bring us closer to the coast of Jericho.

"Ever, it's ok. I can see the shore from here." Mikka's calm voice steadied me. It was just six days ago that he kissed me. He kissed me everyday since. I felt grounded when he was there. I looked up and nodded. I had nothing left right now to say so I smiled. I felt that I would get sick if I even tried to open my mouth again. The rocking was relentless.

"Jericho." Helena shouted. I had never seen Jericho before. After all, it was in a different Kingdom. A Kingdom feared by most. The Kingdom of Melted Cor. A Queen ruled their kingdom ever since the King tragically died, although most people say she actually killed him. I had heard she was unforgiving, and that she literally melted the people that defied her and those that she just didn't like. We did not have time for new enemies now, so we were just looking to go in, find the answers we needed and head back to stop King Jett.

I didn't even bother wiping the tears off my face, it was raining too hard for it to matter anyways. I started to stand up to see what Mikka was referring to. The rocking of the boat almost knocked me off of my feet. He held tight. Fern came up behind me and grabbed my hand. She was so brave and so little, but I was so glad to have her here.

I looked at the shoreline. It was rocky, there were tons of boulders protruding from the ocean below. The waves crashed down onto them as if trying to push them back under the sea. I wondered how we were planning on getting to shore in this storm, but I'd have to worry about that in a bit. My stomach turned again and I leaned off the side of the boat.

Bondi and Gregorio tried to steady the boat, doing their best to turn us to shore. Gregorio was exhausted and couldn't use his gift to push the wind any longer. The storm raged, as if it were trying to punish us. The thunder roared and the lighting surrounded us.

Suddenly, a huge bolt of lightning flashed and the sails of our boat caught on fire. "Everyone hold on!" Gregorio shouted as he tried with the last bit of energy he had to redirect the boat.

The waves pushed us towards the rocks and in the matter of a few seconds, the boat smashed against a rock, cracking the hull of the ship. I tried to hold on, we all did. I screamed for the rest of them "Helena, Bondi, Gregorio, here!" I had tried to get us all together, the boat was going to sink. I didn't know how to swim.

We all held hands as the waves continued to smash the boat into the rocks and we all knew it was over. The side of the boat gave away and we all plunged into the icy cold water. The waves and the current pulled me under, but I would not let go of Mikka and Fern's hands. Everyone was trying so hard to hold on to one another. Helena got up from under the wave to get in a gasp of breath and she started swimming as hard as she could to shore. I kept swallowing gulps of the sea water, causing me to choke.

I could feel the panic attack starting to rear its ugly face. My heart was pounding, my chest was heavy. I let go of everyone's hands. This was it I couldn't swim. I tried so hard to move my arms, but I kept going further underwater. Down, down, down.

Kaitlyn Mueller was born and raised on Long Island, New York. Her love for the outdoors inspired her to move to Colorado where she spent the last 4 years camping, hiking, and backpacking in her free time. Her love for reading has driven her to write her own fantasy series. This particular book was inspired by a backpacking trip through Rocky Mountain National Park. She currently resides with her Husband in Northwestern Colorado with their dog Blue.

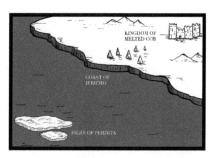

MAP OF THE COAST OF JERICHO